SETTLING DARKNESS

by Paul Heingarten

Published by Decatur Media
New Orleans, Louisiana
www.decaturmedia.com

ISBN: # 978-0-9972626-3-6

Cover design by Y. Nikolova at Ammonia Book Covers

Acknowledgements

To my wife Andrea, thanks for being my compass and for being steadfast by my side for all these years. May we have many more together.

To my friend Lisa Herrington. Your friendship is something I treasure. Thank you for your endless kindness and support, all you have done for me in my writing journey, and for just being a fantastic person. Lisa is a terrific writer in her own right, I encourage you to check out her novel "The Fix" on Amazon.

To Debra Horst. Thank you so much for your kindness and support for me and Andrea. You're a terrific writer in your own regard and I look forward to seeing you published, hint hint!!

To Sarah Lambert-Sheffield. Thanks for your friendship, for beta reading, and for helping me get the word out about this book series, very grateful for you and glad to know you!

To the Bayou Writers Club. Your support and your friendship is invaluable.

To my editor Kit, you've done it again! Thank you for polishing this piece so well, as you have my previous works. You're brilliant.

The term "Hell Hawk" used in this series is derived from the nickname given to several military units during WWII, including the 365th Fighter Group of the Air Force and Marine Fighting Squadron 213. Several members of my immediate and extended family have served in the armed forces, and it is my sincere hope the usage of this term by me in this series is seen as an expression of the respect I have for the military.

Special thanks to my street team, the "Krewe of Paul" for your time, interest and talent in helping me become the best writer I can: Lisa Herrington, B. Allen Thobois, Tanyawriter, Ray Antonelli, Jackie Tansky, Dennis Lavoie

For Andrea. Thank you for loving me for who I am, and in some cases, in spite of who I am.

I love you.

"The night is darkest just before the dawn. And I promise you, the dawn is coming."

(The Dark Knight, 2008)

The story so far…

Ana Crucinal, a twenty-three year old citizen of Lebabolis, has fled her home with members of the Action, the Lebabolis Resistance. The Action has worked to get as many willing citizens as possible to escape from Lebabolis and their cruel structure of forced labor in exchange for a semblance of security and purpose.

Baudricort, leader of the Action, and a former high ranking member of Lebabolis who designed many of its systems, wants to make amends for the destruction his work has done and what it has caused Lebabolis to become.

Ana's brother Varrick, who had joined Ana on the Exodus with the Action, has been kidnapped by Lebabolis, along with a number of the Action who have fallen ill to a disease known as the Pox. Ana made a deal with Baudricort to help him in exchange for a promise to get Varrick and the sick of the Action back.

When a mission to cross time to modern day New Orleans is put in jeopardy, Ana takes matters on herself and flings herself across centuries to find a man they know as Xander Lee.

Xander Lee happens to be the pen name of a man named Nelson Forrester, who lives in early 2010s New Orleans and works on a book about a nation at war known as Lebabolis. After much convincing and some bloodshed, Nelson is forcibly taken to the year 3192 and learns that what he thought was a simple literary project is actually prophecy.

Together, Ana and Nelson navigate the choppy seas of their predicament. They also learn that while they are under the gun, their enemies are closer than they think, and sometimes the best course of action involves joining with the enemy of their enemies.

A deal was struck between Ana and Charista, military leader of Lebabolis, to have the Action join Lebabolis to fight the Omegans, a strange alien race who has marauded the Earth for centuries and has set their sights on the technology Lebabolis has managed to acquire for themselves.

Chapter 1 (Ana)

MY SKIN BURNED at the feel of the sun. The horizon bent upward over us, the walls of the crater we were in swept up like a giant hill. It was a low spot, but it was where the Omegans were headed. Which also made it the one place we had to be.

More of these craters turned up once we got further into the Outlands. Each of them had a giant ball of Valentium at their center and the Omegans were on top of a lot of them, so we had our work cut out for us keeping them away from as much of it as possible.

Three hundred of us filled up this crater. Spread out in a line that snaked up around toward the top of the crater, we stood and watched the Omegans. They'd followed us and fought us wherever they could. It was as much about payback for them as it was their Valentium. The unit we fought in Sector Five turned out to just be a scout. They waited in the wings with three regiments and once they learned what happened it was open season on us, Lebabolis, and anyone else who stood in their way. Kaitlinn and Jason commanded the two legions of troops from Lebabolis and the Action, and I ran this other unit. The plan was to join back up with Kaitlinn and then I'd break off with Nelson and a few others for a run at Cataclysm like we'd agreed.

That being said, we had still been on the run a month since the attack at Sector Five. Charista promised sending help whenever she could in her updates.

Some help.

At least the Action knew more about foraging for whatever we could get our hands on to stay alive and safe. We were the Coalition now, the combination of Action and Lebabolis dedicated to turning back the Omegans. I went back and forth on how I felt about working with Lebabolis, like most of us in the Action did. Charista made a strong play when she used Varrick and our other sick people as hostages so we were convinced. I had every intention that she'd pay for that one day.

People in the Action still considered us separate from the Coalition. We were a band apart, and that was just the way it was. Once we learned about the Omegans and saw what they did in Sector Five, almost leveling the place, we knew that as bad as Lebabolis had been, taking care of the Omegans had to be our number one. So, until the Omegans weren't a problem anymore, we kept in this fight, on Charista's side. I knew though, there'd be a time we'd have to make our move, get our people back who Charista had taken from us and make our own place in this world.

Until then, our agreement was fight to destroy the Omegans, and in return Lebabolis gave the Action its own peaceful existence. But I really wondered if we'd ever go back to anything that resembled peace after this. Charista had us as her army, and I didn't see any scenario that didn't involve her keeping her claws firmly stuck into each and every one of us.

And then there was our deal about delivering Cataclysm to Charista. Nelson and I had that job, and we'd have been well on our way if it weren't for the Omegans jumping our groups every chance they got. They were more after us than Lebabolis ever was.

The Valentium rested at the bottom of the crater. We formed a perimeter around it far enough to be safe but close enough that any Omegan who tried a move was gonna get a little taste of pulse rifle in their face.

The comm was a chatter of people in the crater, also with

some updates from Llewyn. Even though he was far away from here, he still kept an eye on us. His main job though was the move to the Range. His reasoning was it was Baudricort's goal to get everyone there to safety and he was determined to honor his memory, or at least let his idea live until the move succeeded. I had to admit I was happy about it too. Even though he was cryptic with answers to my questions, or just withdrawn sometimes, Baudricort and his presence held it together, held the Action together. The Action he believed in, anyway. A pang hit me whenever he came across my mind, which was pretty regular since he'd died.

I stood next to Treg while we watched the Omegan crafts hovering in the distance. "I don't like this," I said.

"Hey, what kinda talk is that? You're in the Coalition now, remember?"

"We're in a barrel here. Could there be a worse position? They just gotta rain down whatever fire they got and we're toast. So enough of that Coalition talk. It's the Action, and you know it. We're not partners, we're their escorts." I grabbed for a Digiview. "At least we know they won't blow the Valentium up."

"What makes you so sure?"

"Because they'd have done it already?" Even with a superior force about to run hell up our collective asses, a smile found my face. Guess that's what kept me from going full out crazy.

Some others in our group held positions toward the upper edges of the crater for a wider spread of fire. My gaze of our unit, sparse but geared up and ready for a fight, was distracted by the dim glint of gray bands on the arms of the Lebabolis soldiers. Even in this united group, they held onto that one piece of their identity separate from the Coalition, from us as one unit.

Our boots sank several inches into the sand with every step we took, so most people stayed put once they had their spot. We were ready.

Treg exhaled a worried breath. "Think the Hell Hawks can break through up there if we take fire from the Omegans?"

"Whadya mean if? Jacobs is up there. He'll figure out

something."

"Oh, him? I just hope whatever he does won't blow us up too," Treg said.

I never thought of Jacobs as the best pilot in either Lebabolis or the Action as much as he did himself. No matter what, there was never any question that he was the craziest. Rumor had it that on one of his Exodus runs he ran out of ammo and improvised by ramming his Hell Hawk through a detachment of Lebabolis troops. I was glad he was on our side, and I hoped he stayed on the side of the living.

"Jacobs will be busy enough up there." I gazed through the Digiview at the crafts above us. "We got our own party down here too. Whoa, 2000 Omegan troop count? Great."

We'd have been well on our way to Cataclysm by now, but this was another part of our deal with Charista: the Valentium had to be secured and out of the Omegans hands so Lebabolis didn't run short on their fuel supply. We had reserves, but she wanted all the rest kept from the Omegans as much as possible. We wanted them as starved for everything as we were. Only problem with that was it kept us just as stretched out and I worried this all was gonna come down to who had more troops to lose out here. It was Charista's plan, but I wondered just how we'd pull this off.

Side doors on the overhead craft opened and waves of troops dropped from them. Their forms dotted the sky like black rain. They landed on the edge of the crater a hundred yards over and made their way toward us in a slow march.

A gruff voice shattered my already shaky train of thought. "How's it look?"

I eyed Dawn next to me, then returned to the Digiview. I wriggled my shoulder like I had an insect on it, which would've been a lot nicer than her. "Ain't good, but you knew that already."

Dawn had been sent by Charista as my own personal shadow for the trip to get Cataclysm. It was how Charista made sure we, especially me, followed every bit of our agreement. Dawn's one job I could figure was being on my ass every living moment. I was over it and her after the first ten minutes.

She sighed and scratched her arm. "I'm in contact with Charista. She'll send more troops to help."

"When, next month?"

"In time; there's a lot to handle. Jason and Kaitlinn both sent teams to secure some Valentium. Lot better than I can say for our efforts."

I wanted to slam her head with my comm piece but instead turned it on for an update. "Weapons activated and ready; they aren't here to say hey. Stand by with pulse grenades on my go."

This was our routine since Sector Five: run, fight and run some more. For me, it was more than just saving Varrick and the others who Lebabolis had taken from us. I had a promise to keep to Baudricort and to several others among the living.

After just a few months here, I shouldn't have expected the weird feelings to be gone. In very little time, I went from being this brave runaway girl to someone important, at least in a few people's eyes. It all went so fast, I hadn't time to even think about how I wanted this, or even what I wanted here. I'd seen soldiers as a child and young girl; they always seemed so sure of everything. And now I was in charge of this group of soldiers and I gave orders to people, most of them older than me. Their reactions were anything from quiet nods to sidewards glances as they waited for a royal screw up from me. I spoke quick and direct, and hoped the queasy feeling that simmered in my gut each and every day never made it to my eyes.

At least I had one thing protected. Nelson was close in the air with Jacobs. I wanted him out of the way; there wasn't room for anyone who couldn't handle the heavier weapons here. He wasn't much safer with Jacobs, but at least Jacobs could bug out quick if things got terminal.

I felt a sizzling burn on the side of my face closest to the Valentium, which glowed a deep amber. This spot wasn't in any danger of being a Verge site; there was too much Valentium in this one area. But it was a prime target for anyone who needed extra fuel or wanted to disrupt another's supply. Since Sector Five the Omegans showed over and over again that Valentium was their number one. The collateral damage they managed a few times was just a bonus.

I watched the advancing soldiers and thought about our next move. The strategy played in my head a lot. There were so many pieces: the Omegans, the Action/Coalition, Charista, the Valentium, Nelson. It had started right after Baudricort died. Each attack, every move, was like a giant board with pieces everywhere, and I had to figure it out: who to attack first, and where, and how we'd make our way out of our current shit pile. Should have known I was his daughter.

Charista's strategy at least was simple: secure the Valentium and don't let the Omegans get any of it. We needed it for fuel anyway. Supplies were thin, and runs were impossible with the Omegans around every turn. I wished to hell Charista was down here for once. She needed to see how damned tough this battle has gotten. I couldn't let anyone see how I felt, but some days it seemed like a rifle pointed into my mouth would be less dangerous. Lately, we had had to bug out and let them grab more Valentium to save our own asses. We had squadrons of Hell Hawks in the Outlands, but they couldn't be everywhere. We have secured some Valentium already, but this looked like it was gonna be another loss for us.

Our outer positions fired on the advancing Omegans. Several Radomet sprung to action; their mechanical shrieks rang and echoed in the edge of the crater. My fists still tightened at that sound and the memory of when Radomets took Varrick and the rest of our sick.

The positions were a blur of smoke and weapons fire. It was tough to tell which side did better in this fight. Whatever happened, it was up to me to keep as many of our people alive. I dropped down low, my comm pressed close to my lips.

"Central to Wing 7, copy? We need air support, like last week, over?"

A loud thump in front of me shook the ground, and I lurched onto my back. The ships above fired on us as well. "They're crazy; they'll be gone too if any of their shots hit that rock. Don't they know that?"

Treg helped me up. "I wanna know where the hell our air support is." Treg took several aimed shots at the craft. "Remind me to punch Jacobs in the mouth if we make it out of this."

The sky above was peppered with bursts of ship to ship pulse fire. I grabbed for a pulse grenade and armed it when I heard the comm crackle again. "Jacobs, on approach."

"Book it, or there won't be anyone left to rescue!" I yelled.

"They're engaging us up here. I'm circling to the southern side of the crater. Watch for red smoke, then head over."

"Wait, did we check for Darkness yet?" Treg eyed me.

We called it Darkness because there wasn't a better name for it at the time. The Omegans had a device that deactivated our weapons. Vehicles, guns, even lights were shut down by this tech. We'd heard stories about it in the Outlands, but I hadn't seen anything like it yet. It turned up in fights once the Omegan regiments made contact, but so far we hadn't seen 'em where we were.

"I got no clue. Gotta figure they'd have tried it before they sent their troops in for target practice though." A whiff of sand flew up in my face. I swatted my hand and spit the gritty particles out.

More blasts punctured the loose soil and sent it up through the air. I signaled our unit commanders and gave word on the comm to wait for my signal to bolt.

The Omegan soldiers made quick work of the outer positions nearest the crater ridge. The Radomet held up for the most part, but even they had trouble with the larger group that moved through.

Soon we were pushed back within inches of the danger point with the Valentium. The heat on my back intensified and it felt like blisters formed there.

A dull boom rang out in the crater, and a wisp of red smoke billowed from one spot. I almost called out the order to fall back there when several gigantic pops and explosions rang in the sky. The Omegan crafts were jostled but soon steadied out and returned fire on the squadron of Hell Hawks that appeared.

I motioned everyone to the red smoke, and we took off in a

run. Our steps slowed right away, as each time I planted a foot, my boots sank an extra several inches in the sand. When I pulled up, it felt like invisible hands clutched my feet and barely let go. I strained and pushed ahead, my hips sore from the extra work. The pulse fire slammed the ground about us, and we turned and fired at random toward the advancing troops. Five Hell Hawks met us at the end.

I joined the rest of the Coalition troops who returned fire on the Omegans. Once I spun back around and fired on them, I noticed that a group of their troops stopped their attack and focused on the Valentium. I hoped what we did at least gave them something to think about. The Radomet and several other troops showered the Omegans as close as possible without hitting the Valentium store in the middle.

One of the Hell Hawks ascended and shot out of the crater. A group of Omegans broke free and made their way closer to us.

Treg ended up near me. "What's the plan here?"

"Besides not getting our asses blown away? We aren't keeping this one. I'd as soon take off and blow this place from the air than stay here any longer. They'd never let us alone that long anyway. We gotta regroup with a better position. We know where they want to hit; we just have to be smarter about where and when to strike back."

Dawn trudged up beside us. "We can't just give them the Valentium, don't you remember?"

"I remember—"I spun to her—"our number one is keeping our people alive. I'd rather live to fight again. Besides, don't you think it's time we go for the real prize?"

Her lips curled, and she held a glare on me for a long moment. She then lifted her rifle toward the oncoming Omegans. I wasn't sure who I hated more, her or Charista. The fact Dawn was in strangling distance gave her an advantage at that point.

Treg and I were headed for the nearest Hell Hawk when the ground shook under us and sent us sprawling back down, along with a few others. The Omegans made a weird guttural moan and went into some sort of charge. I looked in time and saw a group of them as they pressed forward on us quick. The

Coalition troops shifted; some stumbled in the sand, scurried back and crouched for returning more fire.

Just then, another loud rumble raged above and behind us, the unmistakable sound of hundreds of thunderclaps with an angry turbine wailing through them. I glanced and saw Hell Hawk 42, Jacobs at the helm. Together with the nine other Hell Hawks, they showered the area in front of us. Their barrage tore through several Omegans; the rest pulled back further toward the Valentium.

While three Hell Hawks dropped to a fast landing, the rest stood watch in the air and served up barrages that kept the Omegans from getting closer.

"Everybody, onto the Hell Hawks now!" I bellowed. I twisted myself over and to my feet. Just when I and the others near me made it to the crafts and took off, more explosions slammed the ground. I grasped for the rails and pulled myself into a seat in the rear personnel hold along with the others.

As soon as I was inside, I looked for Nelson but saw no sign of him. I figured he was up with Jacobs with the map displays he checked like he did with the Cataclysm location.

I watched out the narrow windows and saw the rest of the Hell Hawks as they loaded troops and gear and kept as much cover as they could, but the Omegans soon moved up again.

The on board comm crackled to life and I heard that twang voice of Jacobs. "Ev'rybody settle in now. Gonna be a bumpy ride; we're booking out."

The craft lurched about. My gut tightened when I felt us leave the ground, and the wobbling made me nauseous. The angry whine of the turbines built to a shrieking chorus, and I was pulled down into my seat as we rocketed into the air. I grasped the rails near my seat and took a few deep breaths. The nausea that built in my gut was pretty serious. Most of the time I'd flown in these Hell Hawks was for simple transports or quick shots across the border or to another Encampment. Combat flying wasn't something I had much to do with, and I damned well wished I never did.

My eyes focused, and I felt a little better when I saw Treg

across from me.

"They'll let anybody on these things," I muttered.

He smirked a bit. "About time Jacobs got his ass here."

"You seen Nelson? I had him on this one with Jacobs."

Treg eyed the others seated around us. "I saw him loading gear on Hell Hawk 91 when we were scrambling out. Poor guy just had to help somehow."

Nelson had settled down from when he first got here, and he wasn't much for taking off and running wild like before. But the less I knew where he was and who he was with—well, it didn't go so great for Varrick when I had let my guard down earlier.

"So we head to another Regiment?" Treg eyed me.

"It's either Kaitlinn or Jason, and she's a lot closer. The sooner we get back to friendlies, the better."

"Better ditch the Omegans first, or we'll be in even worse shape."

I stuck my rifle between my knees and squeezed the barrel in the hope it made me forget the sharp soreness in my hips. "Yeah, well. And since Charista's running the show, no telling where we'll end up."

"Or how far off track. This is such a cluster. If you and Nelson would've just left earlier, you could've nabbed Cataclysm by now."

"I won't leave troops under attack. I was taught better."

"Glad you paid attention."

"Mmmhmm. It's time we show Charista who's in charge. Not her, not the gray bands."

"Damn right."

"We're the ones who survived on our own, mobile, fighting off their raids on us."

There was never time for plans, with us always being scattered about like this. Only quick discussions, seeds of thought that got scattered to the wind. Our unit and the Regiments of Kaitlinn and Jason were supposed to be the decoys, the interference that drew fire while Llewyn kept the Encampments fixed on Baudricort's plan of moving west while the other two regiments handled defense for Lebabolis. Nelson, Dawn, and I were supposed to make our break for Cataclysm and let the bigger units keep them occupied. But Charista changed her plans from the field, and Valentium became the bigger issue quicker than I thought it would. The hope was we held the Omegans away from Valentium and kept them from getting their filthy hands on the rest of the deposits around. But so far it wasn't working. We were too strung out, and the help they gave was next to nothing.

The ship steadied out a bit and things calmed down. I hoped the queasy feeling in my gut went away soon too. "There won't be a rendezvous if the Omegans zero us in."

A loud explosion pounded the outside of the craft. The lights blinked off, and I felt the craft wobble awkwardly. The soldier to my left jutted his legs out for support.

Treg bellowed. "Ya had to say something!"

"Yeah, well if I knew it was request hour, I'd have asked for food."

The lights went off and flickered back on. The comm came to life again. "Brace for impact, we're hit and going down!"

The craft buffeted and rocked harder, and the lights blinked off again. I crouched down and clutched my legs. I tried to slow my breaths, but it was pointless. The others around me shifted in their seats, and I heard their fast and loud gasps while we tightened our bodies for the crash.

We slammed into the ground with a deep thud. I was jolted out of my seat when the craft came to a stop. The lights flickered off, then back on, followed by billows of smoke in the cabin. "Everybody out before she blows!"

Everyone pulled what they could carry and left the Hell Hawk as it burst into flame. A few grabbed several packs, and we scampered away from it into the woods nearby.

While the others gathered gear into piles, Dawn strode about like she was the commanding officer and expected a detailed report from an imaginary subordinate. She eyed the damaged craft like a mechanic about to enlighten us on how she would've fixed it. She turned to Jacobs. "What the hell was that up there?"

"Excuse me?"

"You heard me, just what do you call that?"

Jacobs narrowed his eyes. "Aerial maneuvers."

"Oh, really? And that includes sending us crashing to the ground?" Dawn closed in on Jacobs, but he just jutted his chest out more the nearer she got. I'd never seen Jacobs strike a woman, but he sure hadn't backed down one inch either.

"Honey, see these people here? I just landed that Hell Hawk safe and kept them from being torched in a burning wreck. All I'm expectin' outta you at present is a thank you while we figure things out."

Dawn's jawbone twitched, and she held her gaze on Jacobs. He returned her icy glare for a moment, then brushed her off and walked around to look at the crowd of survivors as everyone gathered gear from the Hell Hawk. "We walk from here," he said.

"Where to?" I asked out of reflex, but I knew. Jacobs lived for the fight. As much as Treg hated our situation with the Coalition, Jacobs was disgusted we were forced into being escorts for Lebabolis instead of turning our guns on the greater threat.

"We gotta get to a Storehouse." Jacobs face was taut. Lebabolis set up these Storehouses, places for weaponry and gear for any troops of theirs or the Coalition to load up in case of being overrun. They weren't part of the system, so any hacks into MODOSNet wouldn't reveal them. But Warrior Products knew where they were in their sectors; it just meant we had to slip over there to get them.

It wasn't any less risky to head for the Storehouses, but the fact that it meant we would have more weapons made it worth the risk.

While Jacobs checked his P-LAD, Dawn's eyes slid to me. "We have to get to the Capital."

"Are you nuts? Omegans are everywhere. The Capital's gotta be slammed by now. How're we gonna handle Omegans with no ship and just some pulse rifles?"

Her eyes bored into me. "I don't think I need to remind you

about our little arrangement, Ana." She studied a few soldiers who cleared out wreckage and made piles of weapons and stuff they could save.

"Yeah, I know. But that arrangement includes getting our people to safety, and abandoning 'em like this is unacceptable."

Jacobs returned and stood near us. "We're near Sector Three. Figure we can search for it."

"Anybody here from that Sector?"

"No, but it's worth a hunt. I can get this bird up again for a quick hop. The targeting systems could zero it in if they're adjusted right."

I held my gaze on Dawn. "And the Capital?"

Jacobs looked at me a second, then returned to the device. "Uh, at least double that. Day or two, I'm guessin'. Why you looking for the Capital; we gotta get back to our people, right?"

Dawn grasped his shoulder. "Your people will be fine. When we make it to the Capital, you'll have everything you need to help your friends. We better move; time's wasting."

Jacobs eyes slid to Dawn's hand on his shoulder, then he looked at me with a gaze that told me he was anything but the touchy feely type and another collision was coming in seconds.

Chapter 2 (Nelson)

A NA'S WARNINGS HAD GOTTEN easy for me to ignore again. She'd proven to me that this was all real, but that wasn't enough for me to avoid the fights like she wanted me to. But the sight of them flailing through the sand, desperate to avoid the Omegans that pounced down on them like a hungry pack of wolves, just jolted me into action. I leapt out of the craft, pulled people and gear, whatever I could reach, and helped haul things out of there.

The move sped up fast and I got so flipped around while I helped with loading several different Hell Hawks that I forgot which one I rode here on with Jacobs. I felt better when I spied Norg. He and I jumped into the closest Hell Hawk and before everyone was in a seat, we were in the air. I counted thirty total with me before the door shut us into that tight space. The air inside was putrid, like a sweaty gym locker room. No big surprise; as much as we'd been on the run, there wasn't time for things like housekeeping or even baths. I'd have luxuriated in a gas station bathroom right about then and felt like the most pampered metrosexual in this millennium.

Of course, the smell could've just as well been explained by where I was, the personnel hold. We sat fifteen each on two rows of narrow benches held fast against the walls of the ship by seat restraints. I'd been on a few of these so far, and each one reminded me of a cramped city bus, only with minimal windows. One thing I'd learned in a short time was to not stand up too fast or even for too long. These babies were pretty light and those quick dips meant a whirlwind on the digestive tract if you weren't sitting, and sometimes even if you were.

The reduced outside visibility was a blessing anyway. As much as I felt the ship jolt around, if I had the added sight of the spiraling horizon, I would've redecorated the cabin and made the already putrid odor even worse.

I only made out Norg's face next to me on my left. The rest of them were mere shapes with assorted groans and grimaces when the Hell Hawk twisted violently. The craft rocked and rolled like a ride at a fair run by a carny unconcerned with safety. Once I settled into the rhythm of the flight my thoughts went to why the Omegans were there, and I got this really sinking idea that this raid from the Omegans may have been as much about me as the Valentium, even more so. I mean, they had given chase even after we ditched the crater.

I braced myself to stay in my seat while we twisted through the air. The screech of the engines peaked and waned, like the calls of an agitated bird. Outside, random thuds and pops slammed about the walls, roof and floor. My stomach knotted up over the thought at any moment our pursuers could ram a shot right through this thing and kill us in a second.

Seconds later, Zengus' voice came over the system. "Three Omegan birds on our ass; I gotta outmaneuver them. Everybody brace, gonna get rough!"

"What's he mean, get rough?" Norg added his own private concert of groans to his retort and the increased movements of the ride. "Shit, I hate this damn flying junk."

"I thought you prepared for this."

He shot me a perturbed glance. "I was trained to fight on land. Most flights I been on ain't been so damned wild."

My sides ached from holding myself steady for so long. I jammed my eyes shut in the hope my dizziness settled down.

Ana insisted I ride in a ship instead of wait out the ground attack. Said I was too valuable to be killed.

Then I realized that the last thing I'd seen before the doors closed was her, still firing on the troops.

"Norg, did I get on the wrong craft?"

"Long as you wanted 91 you didn't."

A beam of light swung through one of the windows and lit up the sign across from me: tail number 91. "Damn. It was 42. I was supposed to be with her on 42."

"It's fine. You're alive; you made the right choice."

Aside from the pain in my midsection, there was the feeling I'd named the Pull. That was the best word for it, since that's how it felt. Ever since Baudricort hooked me to the Link, I felt this draw to get to Cataclysm. Whatever he did, it awoke something in me, and now I had this constant restless feeling. It was like if I slowed down I got uneasy in an instant, like that top of the roller coaster feeling. The more I headed in a particular direction, the better I felt. I thought for the longest it was just nerves and the rest of the catastrophes I'd been through up to then, but the location on the map, the sight of it just filled me with this urge that whatever I did and however rough it was, I had to get there.

I hauled myself up and peered out the window at Hell Hawk 42 and saw some shots career into its side with an awful noise. I froze and felt a chill on my neck as I watched, helpless. The whine of 42's turbine engines sputtered as if it had pneumonia. The craft spun wildly and dipped lower, and a thick cloud of black smoke trailed behind it.

I glanced at Norg. He just shook his head at the floundering ship. "It's Jacobs; he's got it. He ain't our best pilot by accident." I watched the faltering plane until my vision became cloudy and I zoned out for a second. The rhythmic weaving and bobs of the flight stopped at once and I felt still and calm. I wasn't next to Norg or anyone else, and I wasn't on Hell Hawk 91 anymore either.

A splash of panic hit me. Were we blasted and killed instantaneously? No, this was different. I wasn't in the afterlife.

I was somewhere else.

I saw as clear as I'd looked in the personnel hold seconds

earlier a group of people standing in the woods. Ana was there, and she was face to face with Dawn, the woman from Lebabolis who clung to Ana as part of our arrangement with Charista. I felt an odd sensation around her, but in that case it was more like the feeling of a substitute teacher who eyed me during class.

I saw Ana and Dawn in an argument. I reached out, but I couldn't touch them. Their words were muffled, but I saw their faces, Ana's twisted in anger and the other woman just glaring in response.

Another explosion clanged the outside of the ship. The woods blurred and faded as quickly as they'd appeared, and I was back in the Hell Hawk. The hum and the periodic thunder crash as the engines shifted our position, were overshadowed by a few loud whoosh sounds. Added to the mix I now had the worst pulsing headache I could remember.

"Missiles," a voice muttered. "Won't be missing us much more at this rate of fire."

Norg snorted. "They want payback. You alright, Nelson?"

"Yeah, think so; I just felt woozy."

"Well, you're in good company. Don't worry, Zengus got a few tricks yet, just hope I get to see when they blast those Omegans outta the sky." Norg snarled in contentment. He had taken personal joy in the sight of Ana with Commander Chun of the Omegans when she blasted him into bits back in Sector Five. It rallied everyone in the Action and Lebabolis, but it had brought a hell storm of fire on us for several months now.

The Omegans were strange anyway. The pulls I felt or feelings I got about things like Cataclysm and the Range, and even some people in the Action, didn't happen with the Omegans. They were odd, and the sight of them made me nauseous, but I hadn't figured out why just yet. I'd seen bits and pieces but none of them involved the Omegans.

More rumbles came from outside. I craned my neck for a glimpse through the narrow window. The three ships that careened toward us showed no sign of slowing down. I thought back to how they handled us at Sector Five. They were so clinical about it. They descended on our group like a cheetah toward a wounded gazelle. So ready to accept the surrender that we never gave them. I wondered how much they really knew about Lebabolis, or what would've made them so easily wait for a surrender. I knew I'd been through enough where giving up wasn't an option, and I was damned proud we still had enough who agreed, Coalition or no. It was crazy how that all went down. Instead of blowing us up at first sight, they waited. They didn't fire until we did.

Charista hadn't given us much information since, for someone who seemed like she had a lot of intel on the Omegan threat. The race was on, they were on a spree to harvest as much Valentium as they could find, so Llewyn was also tasked with making quick hits to get the rest of the Valentium available and Storehouse it.

Our options were limited if the Coalition didn't get most of the Valentium first. We had enough for fuel, but moving around more than we ever were, there was no way of guaranteeing this would last.

Zengus' voice burst through again on the speaker. "Norg! Get up here; I need help now!"

Norg released his seat restraint and lunged for the large cabling overhead while he muttered, "Better come too, Prophet Man, in case we need your noodle for gettin outta this."

He stopped after a few steps and looked over his shoulder. "You comin', or you gonna sit there til you puke?"

I followed Norg through several twisted corridors. A blast of hot steam hit me in the face at one point, and I swiped the moisture away. Faded yellow lights near the floor and ceiling lit our way. Now and then I swung into one side of the hull or the other and felt the ship lurch and shake. After more turns, we made it to the cockpit. Out the front of the ship, I saw the horizon twisting about while Zengus pulled and jerked the controls. The console in front of him displayed a map with three red glowing markers. My nausea welled up, so I locked my vision on them instead of the flipping scenery outside.

The muscles on Zengus' arms twitched and bulged as he grappled with the controls. The panel was covered in a wild display of blinking lights and sensors. A lone spark shot out from the center of the console every few seconds. Zengus never even turned his head. "What, ya stop to take a leak? Norg, nav and weapons console. We gotta hit these assholes with whatever this bird's got left. Nelson, to the left behind me, comm center. Raise somebody, anybody friendly. Fast!"

The comm controls lit up and after first glance, I tapped them and opened a channel. "Any idea who's closest right now?"

"Just send a distress call; anyone nearby gets it.

The craft steadied down a bit, but the vibrations from the floor that traveled up my seat through my back, and the high whine of the turbines, gave me an idea of how fast we were going. Zengus swung the controls of the ship about, and we twisted and bucked around.

I shrugged off the chills and turned back to the comm. "Anyone hear me, this is Hell Hawk 91, under fire from Omegans. Need ground to air cover, ballistics, anything, in deep shit, over!" I heard the words spoken in my voice with no hesitation, like a character I watched on screen in a movie.

The ship plunged, and my gut flung up into my throat for a second. Zengus roared and yanked the stick back hard, and we climbed again.

Beads of sweat poured off the back of Zengus' neck. "Can't keep this up. We're gonna be toast. Norg, set a course for us to ditch; least we can take cover in the bush."

The comm console flickered and switched to a map. I felt the familiar tightness in my stomach and thought it was another Pull.

But it stopped.

I tapped random controls on the comm and clung to the hope that someone friendly was nearby. It was possible, but just barely. A few other squadrons of Hell Hawks were in the Outlands, but the Omegans had been around a lot, so they were never in the same area for long.

The comm crackled and a deep voice pierced the white noise. "Stay on course, HH91, salvo loaded and ready."

"Who's there, over?" I tapped the controls, but no other response. "We got company, another unit close by."

Norg looked back. "Who is it? You get an ID?"

"No. They didn't give one."

"What? That's impossible, they ain't gotta give, its tagged on their comm. You sayin' you got a comm with a blank code?"

A few flashes of light and booms pierced the air around us. The ship shook violently and Zengus got to his feet and fought to maintain control. He heaved and wrangled the yoke as if he were a bull rider. His grunts accented the alert beeps from the control panel. His muscles rippled through his shirt and settled once the craft righted itself again. The console in front of him updated, and one of the three red markers disappeared from the screen. The remaining two changed course and headed away from us.

"Alright, 'bout time we get some help," said Norg.

"Yeah but from who? And where?" Zengus answered.

"Ain't gonna be picky over who saves our ass."

"Check the landing sequence, Norg. We gotta land somewhere fast, and it better be close to friendlies."

"No idea," I said. I looked back at the comm, but the screen was blank.

Norg popped up from his seat and leaned across me at the comm. He tapped a few controls. "Now that's strange. Don't see nothin on the register."

"Told you," I said.

Norg climbed back to where I was and pushed me aside. He punched some controls and glared at the screen. "Nah, you don't get it. Anytime someone pops on a comm a tag shows their ID. It's how we know who's sending the info. Lebabolis and the Action tried fakin' that stuff plenty, but no matter what, there's always been some kind of marker. But there's nothing on this one."

"But you heard it, right? Both of you?" Norg furrowed his brow and shook his head as he slid past me back to his seat. I hated that I asked the question, but ever since I was hooked up to that Link, and what I went through when I saw the maps of the Range, I felt more and more tied to this world somehow. I always was, since I'm the one who wrote about it. But now, it was like I was joined with it, like physically. It made me wonder just what other people knew, saw and heard, and what was just in my head. And the vision of Ana and the rest, with no idea of when or even where that took place, made me more worried.

"There are groups in the Outlands, but they've never been loyal to anyone. They're scavengers and stay out of the way."

"You think it was one of them?"

"Yeah, or a Valentium blast. Could be the Verges; they've been unstable since the Omegans started using Darkness."

"No, someone called; that was help from somewhere."

Norg's jaw tightened. "Easy, Prophet Man, you ain't crazy on this one."

Zengus settled back in his seat. "Let's focus. That counterattack could just be a trick to pull us in closer. I'm dropping this bird low and getting cover soon. After we land we locate the nearest Regiment for med treatment and supplies soon or we won't be up for anything else."

Norg tapped the console until several maps appeared. "Kaitlinn's two clicks away; she's got air support capability. Gimme a few minutes to locate their beacon."

While Norg located Kaitlinn's group I thought back about the Pull and the Link. It changed quickly since we teamed up with Charista and the problem went from reigning in the Action to the Omegans. They weren't sending messages anymore. Even the Xander ones weren't a thought anymore. In very little time, they weren't important at all, just a distant thought. I wondered about them and what they would've done to help things out. I guess she wasn't as concerned with the tailored messages once her people and her front yard were part of the war zone. Baudricort's great plan became barely an afterthought, except for his Exodus to the Range. And now here we were, scattered, on the run and under attack. Our only hope was that Llewyn wasn't in a similar spot. At least the groups in the field had the ability and the weapons for fighting back.

These people needed a leader to get them united; that was the only thing that went further than agreeable thoughts and distant shelter at the Range.

The Valkyrie seemed a good bet to me, based on what I'd heard so far. It sure made sense in my book that people rallied around a single person to win their fight. It was more about the Valkyrie than the Link. That work Baudricort had me do seemed like a terrific waste of time once the fighting started for real. He was more concerned about freeing his people; what was he not sharing with us? Why wasn't he more worried about the Omegans? Seemed they were the biggest problem by far. Of course, my Pull hadn't started until he hooked me in, so I wondered if that was his plan after all.

Everything I had heard since I got here told me the Valkyrie was the right choice for Lebabolis to rally behind. But I recalled my hero broke free from captivity. Ana wasn't trapped. She was on the run, sure. No one else had stepped forward, but it was obvious that as much as she was against it, she was the obvious choice.

Ana held true to what she'd said from the start. She wanted no glory or expectations from anyone about who or what she was supposed to be. She led from among the troops and didn't want any grand oath or anything. But once she had Varrick back, she was gone. She had no plans for a monarchy.

The Valkyrie brought a nation together. But what nation? Was it those people with Llewyn, scrambling into the Range to hide like cockroaches? Was it Lebabolis proper, in their ivory and metal tower, hunkered down from the rest of us less than worthy types? Was it the Omegans, who wanted to destroy the Coalition? Why? Were we the evil ones after all?

Being with the Valkyrie also meant swearing allegiance to Lebabolis, and Ana wanted no part of that. I hoped she was OK. She would've sent a comm from her ship by now though. It had to have been her ship that was shot down. Even with Jacobs with them, they were in a world of trouble. They would be flying blind and on foot with the Omegans swirling around like smoke about a campfire.

As far as we knew, Ana was missing, and that didn't set right with me. I had to know she was all right and that crash wasn't the end of her.

As Zengus eased the ship to a dense area of woods, I leaned forward. "Listen, guys, I gotta tell you, we need to watch out for Llewyn."

Norg eyed me. "The hell you talkin' bout now?"

"Look, I know it doesn't make sense. Believe me, I'm not sure why either, but I just got this really bad vibe about him."

Zengus chuckled a bit. "You do realize you're talking about the leader of the Action and the man Baudricort trusted with getting us to the Range."

I shook my head as they shrugged off my statement. I wasn't even sure myself at first about them, but just like I did with the Range and the location of Cataclysm, I felt other pulls about people. It was different with Llewyn. It was a push.

Whatever these new sensations were, there was only one person in the Coalition besides Ana Crucinal I trusted for answers, and I had to get to him as soon as possible.

Chapter 3 (Ana)

DAWN EYED US as if she took some kind of census. Jacobs broke her concentration when he jerked his shoulder and freed her hand from his arm. "I'm helping our people." Jacobs stepped back, the P-LAD pressed flat against his chest.

"We are helping our people." She walked toward him, her eyes narrowed into a stare that danced with Jacob's in a sizzling gaze.

"Our people? Lemme tell ya something, lady." Jacobs thrust a finger in Dawn's face. "Yeah, I know what you're thinking, about Cataclysm. Well, since we got a minute to yap, I figure it's a good time to let you know I think that's BS. Far as I can see, y'all got a piece of meat on a hook for us to grab; what that is, I ain't exactly sure. But a whole lotta us gonna bite it following you before we get there."

I crouched down and traced my finger through leaves and pebbles on the ground. "Why the hell don't we just run and gun for it now? We're thirty strong; we can slip through the other mess in the Outlands."

"You'd die of exhaustion first. You agreed to this deal, you agreed to make this trip; don't get second thoughts now."

"Second thoughts; hell, the whole situation's changed. The Action's been cutting and running on Lebabolis for a good while now. We ain't never needed any help from you before. We gotta take care of our own, because no one else ever did. And that don't include some crazy ole chase into the mountains for your damned secret weapon neither."

The crowd swarmed around Jacobs and broke out in whoops and shouts. Some people yelled out "One or None!" I felt the Action pride burst out in me, but I remembered there was another side to this now.

Dawn's eyes narrowed. I wondered if she even knew how to crack a smile. "You know, the whole purpose of this Coalition was to help each side out. Your people get to stop running like the frightened mice you are, and we get to fight the real enemy without worrying you'll meddle with things and screw them up." Dawn dug her boot into the ground and sent up a brief fountain of leaves.

"I ain't never signed on for ditching my group. Neither did Ana. No way are we leaving anyone behind; the Action's as important as Cataclysm, if not more. One or None, right?"

His eyes found mine, and I saw the fire behind his, raging more than many. He lived that phrase, that rallying cry; so many of them did. There were no gray banders in this group. But for the first time, that battle cry made me ache. It had meant so much for so long, it kept us strong and got us to move and unite. Now with things this backwards, it hurt thinking about it. It was an uncomfortable memory. Did it still mean what it did after what we'd done, and who we'd sided with?

I had no love for Charista, and even less feelings for Dawn, but the deal we made stuck me. They promised protection in exchange for help from Nelson and me. And I just knew, as bad as the Omegans were and as wild as it was in the Outlands, us going it alone was suicide. This decision felt like a blade edged past my ribs into an artery; if I moved or tried to get rid of it, I'd bleed to death.

Jacobs' eyes pleaded with me and held my gaze. His glance said more than his words ever could. It was the same look I'd seen from people in the Action, and a big part of what kept me with them all this time. Even Norg, Kado, Treg and all of my friends from so long ago. They needed me here. They'd have done the same for me, and it was a safe bet the rest of our group from the Crater were looking for us right then. And Varrick, could I walk away from him being cured? If only we had left sooner. Was I really a leader, when I hadn't been able to even decide what was best for me and my own brother? Now we were ditching the Coalition, including our people, when they needed us most. Why didn't they deserve the same respect? Besides, at that point, "anyone in the Coalition" included Nelson, who I wasn't leaving behind to be stranded or hurt by a damned sight. Crazy as he was, Jacobs would've died before he let anyone else in the Action get hurt. And that went over and beyond the damned Coalition.

Jacobs was spot on about our situation: with no ship and minimal guns, we were an easy target no matter where we went. Hell, the Omegans may not even have to fire a shot if one of these roving bands in the Outlands got to us first.

I had this awful idea that Nelson was dead, but only for a few seconds. They hit us so hard in that escape, I had to think that others out of the ten took fire too. As images of Nelson among the wounded came into focus in my mind, I shook myself to get that thought away. *No, you'll crumble if you start thinking like that. Keep it together. People are watching you.*

Pulling my shoulders back, I clutched a rifle behind my shoulders and enjoyed the cool metal against my neck. I chuckled to myself when I recalled how Treg held his rifle the same way. My mind wandered to the options. Thanks to Jacobs and Dawn's quite clever yammering and insults, they were clear cut. I wondered if that was how I sounded during those fights I'd had with Baudricort, over questioning Encampment moves and arguments for more rations, or later on with ideas on securing the Action from raids. I gathered a slow breath in my lungs and imagined Baudricort. When things got rough since he died, it helped when I pictured him, like he wasn't dead just yet; he was still here, my father.

When I did that and spoke, the words came through me, and I felt my father's presence. "Jacobs is right. Making our way to the Capital over open ground with no protection is very dangerous. Not even Dawn can deny that."

Dawn shook her head. "It's not a question of denying. You made a deal and you have to honor—"

"If we get to a Storehouse, we have a chance." Jacobs interrupted.

"Hell, we could even split up, send a smaller group back to the Capital and send another group back to the fight," I added. Jacobs nodded, a smile creeping on his lips.

Dawn seethed. "That's not what we agreed to."

I swung the rifle to my side. Dawn tensed up when the muzzle moved past a straight line toward her chest. "Neither was getting shot down. What's your background, anyway? You a Warrior Product over there, 'cause it looks like they laxed requirements letting your flabby arm twitchy ass in."

She straightened herself and looked three inches taller. "I'm an Intellectual. And you're what, a Worker?"

"Had me some after school learning. You had it cushy with the Lebabolis elite. Out here, things happen and we deal with 'em. We make hard choices and handle the fallout. We don't always like it, but we go with what we're dealt. And we take care of our own. That's what the Action's about."

"There is no Action." Dawn returned a triumphant smile.

"Bullshit," said Jacobs.

"Where there's two or more of us, there's always an Action." I glared at Dawn.

"Our people are in danger, and we have to make sure they're OK. There were ten Hell Hawks in that crater. We don't know what happened to the others." Jacobs steeled his gaze for a moment. "And there's also the Guard. Maybe we can reach them."

The Guard was the elite unit of the Valkyrie. I hadn't heard anyone mention them out loud, but plenty wondered about the roving bands in the Outlands and the chance some of them were linked to the Guard. Nothing was ever known for sure; it was just a lot of interesting stories so far.

I held back a chuckle when Jacobs mentioned them. It was

better having Jacobs on your side in a fight, but still sometimes he talked crazy even by his standards.

Dawn scoffed at Jacobs. "The Guard? You don't put faith in that decrepit band of warriors, do you? Calling them warriors is a stretch. You realize how long it's been since they've been any kind of formidable unit?"

"Don't matter, they're around."

"And just how do you know?"

"I've heard things."

"Oh, things. Like rumors? Fairy tales?"

I wondered what Jacobs knew. There was the Valkyrie emblem, but I was always told even talking about the Guard was forbidden. The unit only lived in memories of some older Products and random whispers around the Sectors.

"I ain't seen any proof they're gone for good, and the way they gave y'all hell back then tells me they're tough, and toughness means survival. You ask me, they're just what we need now."

Dawn shook her head. "We're low on time. As much time as we just spent talking about long lost warriors, we could've made good progress to the Capital."

"Well, just what are we getting there? Can't you clue us in so we know why this trip is so damned important?" I asked Dawn.

"Because no other way will get us there. We'll never make it on our own, not even if that Hell Hawk is flying and piloted by Captain Ego over there. You don't understand; you're trying to win a battle, I'm trying to win the war," Dawn said.

"By gettin' Cataclysm. Now who's believin' in fairy tales?" Jacobs rolled his eyes.

Dawn's gaze flopped back between Jacobs and me. "It's not like that."

I waved Jacobs off for a second. "So far it's more like a hunch, but y'all kinda got me and the Action where you want us. So again, what is so damned special at the Capital that's more important than Cataclysm now?"

Dawn eyed us and those who stood close. She hesitated, but then after she weighed out the risk of telling it, she took a deep breath. "Charista's promised us transport ships. Very sleek, very fast. They have a good chance at outrunning the Omegans. They won't outgun them, but with their speed, the Omegans won't have time to get a fix on us. But they're only in the Capital. We can't get to them anywhere else, especially not via a Storehouse."

"What if the Omegans hit it with their Darkness? They've already downed Hell Hawks with it."

"I grant you there's no guarantee with the transports either, but they've got a lot better chance than Hell Hawks; they're much faster. If we want a fighting chance at this objective—"

Jacobs had been leaning against a tree, his arms folded tight while Dawn made her case. But when she brought the transports up, he lit up like a case of explosives. He shoved off from the tree, his face twisted in a sour look, and he waved his hands about as if he were fanning the reek of Dawn's putrid idea. "Just hold it, now she's yapping about transports. Multiple, right? We been scratching and crawling like dogs to get to the Range in those land clunker facilities. Why the hell she been saving them til now? We're getting picked off—"

"We don't have enough ships for the Coalition. They're advanced prototypes, and right now Charista wants them used only for the Cataclysm run. This is just a backup plan." Dawn's lips drew in a line.

I knew the burning in my gut was there to stay until we at least knew about the rest of our people. I thought Nelson would've been safer away from me. After Baudricort was killed I thought whoever did that might come after me, especially if anyone else knew he was my father. I was glad Nelson wasn't there with me then. Just maybe he had a better chance than us.

Jacobs made his way around to the others, talking to them two, three or more at a time. Their eyes warmed to his words, and I saw their nods and curious glances my way.

I adjusted my comm for the ship Nelson was on but got no response. I dropped slowly to the ground and watched the comm as the sounds of Jacobs and Dawn arguing faded into the background.

I went to a nearby hill with Treg as he still maneuvered the P-LAD for a signal to locate the Storehouses. Even if we split up, it was up to Jacobs to give coordinates to the Capital for Dawn and whoever else attended there.

Dawn's voice surged to a shout. "Each of you is in debt to Lebabolis! You don't know what happens if you just go renegade."

"I'll entertain your crazy ass theories another day, lady," Jacobs muttered. He planted his feet, a defiant sneer on his lips.

Dawn's eyes widened, and she looked ready to unload a verbal salvo at Jacobs, but she never got to. Hell Hawk 42, already damaged from our narrow escape from the Omegans, exploded. The blast knocked several others and me down and sent the trees into a spastic, angry dance. The rattle of leaves hung in the air along with a steady column of smoke from the wreckage.

A loud ringing clouded my hearing for a few minutes, and I gagged on the odor of burning fuel and mechanical ship guts. People staggered to their feet in a daze, and if I had been alone I would have seriously doubted I'd just seen this. But it was real.

Shouts came into focus, and a few people rushed over to some who stood close enough to get hit with the flames.

Others scrambled to their feet. The moans and grumbles gave way to shouts toward the ship.

There it was, left in a smoking smoldering mass of black twisted metal. Any hopes we had of getting it flying again were gone. A mangled number 42 was most of what was left of her tail. There it lay, like a dead animal. What had kept us from being vaporized a little while ago was quickly burning down to embers and jagged pieces of metal.

I jumped up and hauled whoever I could grab away in case of a secondary blast. We settled back and collapsed again to the ground fifty yards away from the burning wreckage. I scanned the group until I saw Jacobs. His eyes had widened, but a clear spike of rage blossomed. He swung his rifle up and took a few steps toward the simmering wreckage, then turned to Dawn, his lips pursed. "What did you do?"

"Excuse me?"

"You heard me." He approached her; his rifle came to a bead on the center of her chest. "You tryin' to do us in over here; what the hell you pulling trying to blow us up?"

"Hold on; what even makes you think I'd do that? I was on that ship just like the rest of you. You really think I'd kill myself?"

"No, but you'd keep us from taking care of our own. You weren't getting takers on your Cataclysm mission, and we need a ship for gettin' back to our people. Not having one's the best reason to go 'long with you to the Capital."

"Might've been a fuel leak; did you think of that while showboating and playing hero?"

"I call it savin' your Intellectual Product ass, honey." His face twisted. "I got an idea." He powered up his pulse rifle. The whine of his weapon as it came on to firing mode froze everything in place. My breaths stopped. I felt Treg's hand on my arm, but my entire body was stuck in place. He ran over to Jacobs and Dawn.

While I watched the scene between the three of them, a weight pressed on my chest. I let out a sharp gasp, but no one noticed. Then, I heard a voice that sounded hollow with a slight echo.

+Ana.+

I glanced around. My fists clenched at the sound of my name. For a second I thought it was the Comm, but no, that was still dead.

Then I remembered.

It was the voice I'd heard before, at the Verge site and when I made my trip back to 2014. I hadn't heard it since, but it was impossible to forget. And it wasn't the Link either, like I'd thought it was once. It echoed in my head, and my thoughts became a voice in response.

Hello?

+I need your help.+

You're the one who called out to me when I went through the Verge?

+I am.+

The memory of the voice made my throat tighten, but I wasn't speaking out loud.

Who are you?

+It's not important. But you must get to the Lebabolis capital as soon as possible.+

Why? What about our people?

+They are fine.+

Nelson?

+Yes, of course. They found help and are safe for now.+

I can't; there are Omegans everywhere.

+What's at the Capital will help you defeat them. Please, you must go there.+

We're alone, with hardly any weapons. We'll be picked off.

+Do what you always do... find a way.+

We have to arm up first.

+Be quick. Someone there needs you. Someone you care about.+

Then, along in the background, I heard another voice, a young boy pleading in wails of pain.

"Varrick?" I blurted the name out in a quick sob. Dawn swiveled toward me.

+Yes. Make your way to the Capital; it's urgent. Take a small group. No more than four people. Scans might not pick you up. They look for larger units.+

The weight released off me, and my hearing cleared again. There was Jacobs, his rifle poised now at Dawn's head. Beads of sweat squirmed across and down his forehead.

Treg hollered, but Jacobs stood fast. The muscles on his arms bulged, and I realized why Treg hadn't grabbed the rifle. It was set to fire, and if he missed when he reached, Jacobs might've set it off, even just as a nervous flinch. In spite of this, Dawn wasn't fazed; at least she didn't show it. Her eyes were as cold as a Radomet visor. For once I had to admit I had just a sliver of admiration for her.

I marched up past Treg and stood between Jacobs and Dawn so the rifle was pointed at my chest.

Jacobs' face flashed in confusion. "What the hell you doing,

Crucinal?"

Treg reached for my arm. "Ana, get out of—"

"No!" I swung away from Treg. "Go ahead, Jacobs. You wanna kill somebody? Shoot me."

The sweat came quicker down his forehead. I heard Dawn behind me say, "It's a wonder you people survived this long on your own."

I swiveled my head over my shoulder. "Dawn, shut the immediate hell up." Looking back to him, I said, "Jacobs, don't waste time on her. You want to get to our people, rejoin the fight and keep the Action safe. It's what Baudricort wanted, what he still wants. His dying wish was for our safety. You know we made this other deal with Lebabolis to keep that going. So I'm going with Dawn to the Capital to finish our part of it."

"Oh, are ya now?"

Jacobs stared at me in disbelief. I stared at the three orbs, the angry glow of Jacobs's rifle and his eyes that struggled to make sense of what I meant.

"It's what separates us from them. We finish what we started. We promised Lebabolis we'd go for Cataclysm, and that's what we need to do."

He lowered his rifle. "You realize you're going with the person who just tried to kill us?"

My stomach knotted when I realized I had no good counter to that. "Yeah, well, she needs me as much as she thinks we need her, Jacobs. She knows her big boss wants me alive and I've got a deal with 'em, so if anything happens to me it won't be pretty for her." I turned to her. "Isn't that right, twitchy?"

Dawn nodded.

"And I'm looking out for who we left back there too." My gut tensed when I thought about Nelson and what they may have ended up with. Maybe they weren't even as lucky to have landed as we were. They could've been captured.

He shot a glare toward Dawn, and to me a concerned look. "They'll use you and spit you out when they don't need you no more."

"I'm a soldier, and I'm completing my mission. You take care of our own and get our people safe."

Jacobs' eyes pleaded with me more, and I felt my throat hitch. "If you see Nelson, tell him I'll see him soon." The words came out half as a request, half as a sob.

"Tell you what," Dawn said. "Jacobs, you want to leave, go right ahead. That goes for the rest of you too. From what I've seen on the tracker, it won't be long before you get snatched up by an Omegan patrol or worse, and so help me I won't feel bad in the slightest."

"Back at ya, sweetheart. I'm bee lining for the Storehouses and getting back in this game." He glanced at the rest who'd gathered around us. "Anyone who wants to save our people, come with me."

That was it. Our Coalition group may as well have reverted to Action at that point. The crowd made their way around Jacobs until Dawn, Treg and I were the only ones standing apart.

"We should stay in a small group." I grabbed my rifle and powered it down. "We'll move quicker. Jacobs needs a lot of muscle if he's gonna scrounge for a Storehouse."

Dawn checked her P-LAD then nodded. "Fine. Ana and I will do it."

"And me," Treg said as he walked closer. He winked at me and hoisted his rifle.

I looked into his eyes. A trace of the fierce calmness remained, but a glint of worry pushed through.

"I've had your back until now; not stopping anytime soon."

I offered him a smile in return. While the group with Jacobs passed around weapons, he approached me and nudged a pulse pistol into my hand. "In case."

"Thanks."

"Your old man was pretty hard headed too. Guess I shouldn't be too surprised."

"Yeah, well. Take care of yourself."

"Damn straight. And you, don't turn your back on her, you or Treg. You're out there walking through the woods, got to take a rest, even for just a second, she may get one on you. I mean it. Don't think she can't call out a squad with that P-LAD of hers neither."

Treg nodded. "Jacobs, link back up with Kaitlinn when you can, give her our update. We'll reconnect as soon as possible."

Chapter 4 (Nelson)

THE REST OF THE HELL HAWKS that made it out flew off to the rendezvous point. We arrived in time to see the sun sinking below the horizon. It cast a deep amber hue on the sky, but we had no time for scenic pictures, much less the gear to take any. Six out of the original ten ships made it back. We stood around and checked for who was safe or not. The ships wheezed black smoke as their engines purred to a low hum as they were powered down.

Kaitlinn's regiment still had a decent number of troops, over a thousand at that point. The landing strip was a carved out section in the wilderness. Trees formed a jagged border that gave little protection other than an indication of where the rendezvous area ended. Toward the center of the clearing, next to the landing area was a familiar sight, the temporary buildings used for troops and storage. What Llewyn's group hadn't used in their trek to the Range was left behind to help the Coalition troops in fighting the Omegans and keeping their eyes off the main group headed for safety.

"Checked troop counts on the console before we landed and we got 1800 total here. Not bad. Just hope the rest of our wing didn't get zapped like 42."

"How about the others, like Jason?" I asked.

"He's railing it up north. Giving the Omegans some shit

alright, but we hadn't heard much from him so far. Gotta think, hard ass crazy dude like that, he'll be alright. He's wild but he ain't stupid."

The whines of the Hell Hawk engines reverberated against the tree line like squawks from an agitated pack of birds. Waves of heat and engine exhaust splashed my face, and I coughed at the noxious fumes while I watched Zengus and Norg with the others. The soldiers checked on the wounded while some made adjustments to the Hell Hawks.

A group of thirteen Radomets kept a silent watch over the scene along with a collection of Coalition gray band troops. They strode the outer perimeter, the Radomets' mechanical gait almost humanlike, but with enough awkward jerks that reminded anyone they weren't human. Radomets were around and provided security here, and where they could. They just weren't able to handle the unstable terrain like the crater. Too bad; we could've really used them there.

This was a temporary fall back, according to Norg. Kaitlinn wanted time to regroup, as little time as they could grab. Even I knew we had to hit them with an even bigger force than we had here. Kaitlinn's regiment had a good punch, but without word from Jason she wasn't about to get into anything too deep in case we had to fall back to Lebabolis for a final stand.

Or head to the Range.

I wondered how it would go down if it meant protecting the Range or Mother Lebabolis, and then I realized it was obvious. We were as much on our own as we ever were if this came down to survival.

If Jacobs somehow made it up with Jason, and Ana was there, they'd be fine. I hoped she'd be alright wherever she was, but I wasn't too sure. The Pull was the only thing I'd been 100 percent on of late.

Once they saw who made it back from the Crater attack, the next step was getting back in the fight. The longer they stayed here, the more time the Omegans had to find Llewyn's group and pick them off for good.

Coalition troops hurried around the place. Some tended to the mobile facilities while others counted and checked weapons and the rest took care of the injuries in a makeshift field hospital. Wounded were directed to a med station for treatment. The whole scene felt like a busy airport or better yet, a disaster scene. Soldiers reached for equipment and shouted updates to others. Medics raced about the wounded.

I grabbed Norg. "You tried raising Jason on the comm?"

"Comms are spotty as hell. Can't even get advisories from Lebabolis right now, and that's a real bite. We're bloody and blind out here. Best we can do is hope we get word from a scout unit before another company of Omegans rolls over our asses."

"What about those guys who called our ship?"

"No idea. Let's see if Kado can figure that out. If he's even here."

Norg and Zengus joined in with the work on the Hell Hawks. The bold ships had a continuing purpose: provide whatever air support they could and keep the Omegans focused on them and not the ground troops. We had a small edge on them in the air, not with guns, but with maneuvers. And some help from other Coalition soldiers on the ground.

I left the group of soldiers that tended to Hell Hawk 91 and headed toward the med station when I heard a gruff voice over to my side. "Hey, gimme a hand over here!"

After a second I found the source. Two Coalition soldiers knelt over a third, who looked about the size of the other two combined. The soldier who called to me had a bleeding gash under one eye.

When I got closer, I saw the man on the ground they surrounded. He writhed in pain, and I felt my legs tense at the gaping wound in his midsection. A strong wave of nausea hit.

"I- I'm not a medic, fellas."

"Don't matter, let's move him to a table. Medics are too busy; help us out, huh?"

Eye Gash directed me to one side of the man while the other soldier, a taller thin man with glasses, cradled one of the man's arms. With some effort, we heaved and got the heavy guy onto a table. Heavy Guy groaned loudly and some blood splashed on my arm. I felt woozy, as much from the blood as the heavy lifting.

Eye Gash looked the man over, his mouth crinkled and his eyes stained with worry. "Hell of a damned war, ain't it?"

"Oh yeah. I'm Nelson, by the way."

"Lon. This one over here's Tayl and the wounded fella down here's Mack."

"Nice meeting y'all, aside from the circumstances. Don't suppose you know where I could find Kado?"

Tayl's voice was gruff with a slight gurgle of someone with a lung ailment. "Haven't seen him since we got here yesterday."

"If he's here, check the med station. He's gonna be pretty damned busy if he's around though, unless you been shot or worse."

"Thanks."

The med station was in total chaos when I got there. Two tables staffed by three people tended to twenty soldiers. Scattered around were bodies of those with serious wounds in various states of consciousness and life. I noticed two of them marked with the symbol that indicated they had Pox. It reminded me of Ana's brother Varrick, and made me wonder how he was, in the involuntary custody of the Lebabolis government. I thought about Charista's pledge to Ana, part of what started this whole Coalition thing, and wondered if she really could have cured the Pox in them.

Bandages were flung about like Mardi Gras parade throws while the medics worked at a frantic pace. One girl medic got close to me on her way through the crowd, where she did quick assessments of the soldiers, so I grabbed her shoulder. She jerked her head up and spun around, a scowl on her face.

"Don't touch me like that, or you'll get a hypodermic in the eye."

"Sorry. Is Kado here?"

She huffed and returned to her P-LAD, her head nodding. She shot me another nasty look before she bothered with a response. "Negative. He's doing a job for Llewyn."

"Where?"

Her eyes tipped upward to me, and her scowl deepened a bit. "Can't you see we're busy? Ask Kaitlinn."

She continued her work without another word in my direction. Even if some of them had an idea about what happened to me with the visions, there was no way any of them checked me before the wounded. What I had was filed under "Crazy". They had enough cases of "Dying" for a good while.

I trudged back toward the mobile buildings and caught sight of Kaitlinn. She held a P-LAD tight beneath her folded arms. Her broad shoulders were a random but distinct reminder of how small mine were in comparison and how I needed to find whatever gym these people used around here. I made a personal note if I ever got back home, I was gonna start a dystopian warrior workout as my surefire crazy rich retirement plan number 793.

Kaitlinn alternated between gestures to soldiers. She directed them like a seasoned symphonic conductor and gave a stoic survey of the scene of casualties between batches of orders to her subordinates. Just the sight of Kaitlinn gave me a feeling of calm. I couldn't imagine what her inner dialog was, but on the outside she looked like a battle tested general. She reminded me a little of that General Honore guy I'd seen as a kid in New Orleans after Katrina. She grasped her ear comm and rattled off lines of crisp clear orders then returned to the scene before her.

"How goes the war?"

She spun to me. From the first time I'd seen her, Kaitlinn had this ever annoyed look on her face. I figured if she ever cracked a smile, that was the moment I would drop dead from surprise. Her battle armor covered most of her body, and jagged scratches and some charring canvassed a good bit of the armor. She was the leader of the field troops. She came from the Lebabolis side of course, and while the Action didn't think as much of her for it, they weren't saying too much about it either. Of course, the sideward glances I noticed from the Action troops made me realize just how little they really thought of her. Like her or not though, she was in charge of the field, she and Jason anyway.

Every time she looked at me, her eyes got this weird glint as if her brain conducted some elaborate analysis of my exact purpose on this planet, with results that were so far inconclusive. Her green eyes pierced mine like a bird of prey. They reminded me of Ana's, but instead of how Ana's glance made me speechless, Kaitlinn's visage made me feel like I was under inspection from a superior officer, or even an interrogation.

"Ah. Mr. Forrester. Glad you made it out." Her tone was as flat as an empty balloon. At least with Baudricort, I gathered he was kinda interested in what I had to offer, or at least that I was around. With her, it felt like she waited for an opportunity to hand me over for ransom. She was the last person I ever wanted to play any kind of card game with. Some of her looks I swore I'd gotten from an irate Bourbon Street bouncer or two.

"What happened in the Crater?"

"We were overrun and outnumbered."

"What do these Action people think they can do?"

"If we hadn't gotten out when we did, we'd be dead. We got off some shots at them; Ana had us there."

"Ana Crucinal; yes, I know her. The darling of the Action, an untested, illegally trained Deviant. As if I didn't have enough problems on my hands, I have to deal with somebody's messiah complex."

"She's not about that."

"I'm not so sure. Anyway, poor planning and execution. If we weren't so stretched out, I'd have sent a group there myself. That's the problem letting ragtags run the show."

Kaitlinn had gotten a lot of attention earlier in the war, after the attack at Sector Five, by leading early maneuvers and turning back a division of Omegans from the Capital. It got harder and harder to keep the Capital safe, though. The Omegans had more numbers, and they forced the Coalition of Lebabolis and the Action into a regroup. The hope was this group with all Lebabolis' strength and all the Action's resourcefulness had what it took to finally stop the Omegans. Until we got Cataclysm, anyway.

Kaitlinn glanced back at her P-LAD and spoke into her comm again. She watched the Hell Hawk crews and the rest of the troops. Her feet planted as if they were two tree trunks, she stood firm and resumed her meditative stare from a few minutes earlier, the kind of trance I pictured reserved for the likes of Napoleon Bonaparte or Catherine the Great. I imagined she had a lot on her mind, and since Baudricort's murder was still a mystery, I assumed she was wary about the same thing happening to her.

No one ever discussed what had happened to Baudricort in recent months, or if anyone had ideas, they hadn't shared anything with the group. It really bothered me how they never told me here. It wasn't like I knew a whole lot about what they had planned, but still... being this much in the dark had me pretty worried. With nothing they could use for information in their fight, I was that much easier for them to take out, so they had one less thing to worry about if I wasn't around.

"Should've gotten more Valentium," she blurted out loud to no one. "We've got to be better about that. These vehicles don't power themselves, and the raids are getting more dangerous by the day. The Omegans are sealing off the Valentium one site at a time; we can't keep letting them take it."

I hated the way she brushed off what we were up against. "It's been a rough fight. Has anyone else been able to get some Valentium?"

"Of course we did. Our Warrior Products were trained more for engagements than Ana's group."

"They hit us pretty hard back there. Their force was ten times what Ana had there, easy. But we had other help once we left the crater."

She raised an eyebrow. I nodded and continued, "Somebody shot down a few of those Omegan crafts chasing us. Was that you or someone else from the Coalition?"

"No, I'd have heard if it was. Could be Jason's Regiment, but more likely it was one of the renegades. I wouldn't be too thankful. They could've easily shot you down instead."

"I assume you heard about Jacobs' group."

"Mmm. That's going to hurt. Jacobs is a good man, even if his loyalties are skewed." Kaitlinn served the praise up with the ease of someone who had a gun pointed at their head. "I understand Ana was on that flight too."

"Yeah. Heard anything from them?"

"Their beacon showed a safe landing; that's what we know. The signal went dead not long after."

"Oh?"

"It could be their attempt to avoid tracking. We're trying to raise them on the comm, but that's tricky." Her eyes darted past me and without another word, she walked toward a group of Hell Hawk pilots and briefed them.

Just past where Kaitlinn and the pilots stood, a large procession of troops formed and loaded wounded personnel and gear onto the mobile facilities. I may not have been around here long, but I was familiar with this sight: another Relo.

Kaitlinn's discussion continued with the small group, but the mechanical gasps, whirrs and other sounds that came from close by muffled most of it. The troops in her presence, however, stiffened up and regarded her with complete attention and silence. I smirked at the sight of the gray bands on most of her rapt audience. No wonder she won them over so well. She was one of Charista's best senior officers, and the more I saw her with her troops and how she and they got along, the more I saw, not just felt, what had been happening. Ana had been worried how much these two groups had really meshed, and I didn't blame her at all. I wished I knew where she was; the longer I stayed with Kaitlinn, the more I felt like a prisoner than an ally.

I knew I wasn't the only one who felt that; Ana was never that sure of Kaitlinn either. I wondered if my whole separation from Ana in the crater was part of some attempt to get me away from Ana and even more vulnerable.

I missed Ana.

The hurricane I'd entered when I got here hadn't stopped, and the damage it did hadn't happened all the way yet. The people on my team were few. Ana had my back, but her being gone made me rethink what I needed for my best shot at survival and one day getting out of this. I had the Pull, and if I could just figure out how to control or at least get back to following it, maybe I had something. I knew, just from the look in Kaitlinn's eyes when she watched me, it wasn't a good idea to share too much about the Pull too fast. I mean, I had trusted Baudricort much more and he damn near cooked my brain on that Link machine. They had the Link, they had their weapons, but information was mine and I had to watch how I used it. Without Ana nearby, my back wasn't covered, so I watched my mouth instead.

The word from several people back in the Crater was Llewyn needed another two weeks if they didn't run into any other problems or attacks. And that was one of our main goals: give the Omegans a target to shoot at. Maybe we took a few of them down in the process. I thought about my primary mission, getting Cataclysm, and how Ana and I were not on track for that.

I caught up again with Kaitlinn and her gray band cult as they were planning the Relo and their next move after that. When she noticed me in the crowd, she frowned and began using code that I didn't understand. But I definitely got the message that she wanted me gone, someway somehow, even if it came down to shooting me in the head.

I'd never missed home more. Little stupid things that I'd had, food, friends, even a cashier at the supermarket, any one of them right then and there would've made me relax if just for an inkling.

And of course, I wanted to know about Dad.

The road home was further and further away; it seemed like the grainy distance on a highway road, flickered in the distance just out of my reach. The Verge, the break in time that got me here, was thrown out of whack according to what had Kado told me back in Sector Five. As much as he knew about a lot of things, he hadn't come up with any solution to that, which worried me the most.

My gut ached at the thought of how long it had been since I left 2014 and what he must have gone through ever since. As my mind played back more memories, a stiff pain shot through my neck. I grasped for the small control device. Kado had developed it as a way to slow the effects of the Verge on me. It worked alright, except for feeling like I was being strangled every now and then. I was about to ask Kaitlinn where Kado was when I noticed her staring at me.

"Something wrong?" I asked.

She said nothing but watched me for a little while longer. I felt a lump form in my throat and swallowed to relieve the tension. It didn't help, so I tried my other option. "I'd like to see Kado. Any chance you can point me to where he's at right now?"

She arched an eyebrow. "Kado? Why do you want to see him?"

"I'm having problems with the device he gave me, I'd like him to look at it."

Her brow creased and she gave a quick sigh. "Our wounded get treated before we move out again. I can't let this large a group sit too long. I'd have moved much sooner if we didn't have this many injured. Besides, Kado's not here now anyway."

"Can you get me to him?"

"No way."

"Why?"

She faced me. "Because for reasons I'm sure I don't know fully, Charista considers you valuable. And with Omegans running wild over most of the Outlands and inside Lebabolis borders, I won't risk an asset because of minor discomfort. You read me?"

Dread settled on me like a spring rainstorm.

An asset?

My throat clenched, but then the irritation spiked. I narrowed my eyes toward her.

She responded with a glare of her own, as if she'd read what I was about to say. "I know your worth, Nelson, trust me. I'm capable of reading briefings."

"Alright, so then how the hell do you know how bad this problem I'm having is or if it won't get worse?"

"People are dying here, Nelson. We're still getting Pox outbreaks. We tend to the most pressing issues first. You'll hang on with this device, and we'll get you to Kado when we can."

Her eyes burned back against my stare. A soldier ran up to her with an update, and she took off with him. Yeah, my second class citizen status has been reconfirmed in spades.

I watched the loading in progress for a few more minutes, and Norg approached. "There's scout patrols around; we're waiting on their latest reports from the Omegan movements. We're rotating out in a day or so."

"Where to? Anywhere near a beach?"

Norg laughed. "Not quite. But I'm thinkin' I need to see Kado. Heard he's working on new weapons powered by Valentium. More powerful than we've ever had before, and we'll need 'more powerful' if we're gonna get an edge on those Omegans."

"You going? Kaitlinn told me no."

"Why?"

"Said it's too risky."

"She's not wrong, but that never stopped the Action before." Norg smirked, and a twinkle appeared in his eyes when he said Action.

"I'm all in. This thing on my neck is bugging me."

"I'll make it happen."

"Kaitlinn won't like that," I said.

"Duh. Ana can't have all the fun, right?"

I laughed. "What about Zengus?"

"Nothing doing; he's been reassigned to a flight squad. But me, I'm not gonna sit on my ass and wait. I'm a Warrior Product. We don't wait for an opportunity, we make one."

The ships were scattered about on the pad, an uneven display of firepower. While most Hell Hawks were worse for wear, the soldiers worked on them and loaded them up before the temporary encampment was broken down for their next move.

Most of them did nothing that made me feel like I was at home, but after a few surly looks and snarling rebukes from Norg I realized that he'd given me as close to a welcome as anyone. Even after what happened when we lost Otto, Ana, Norg and their Circle never held it against me, no matter that I'd taken off running and put them in a bad spot earlier. I guess they realized that just like them, I wanted to win this fight.

Kaitlinn marched about the temporary facilities while they were closed up, and I mused that she looked for a place I could fit, some kind of compartment so this 'asset' would be kept tidy and clean, like a crate of water.

She'd always kept me on the outside of her group, and at every turn I knew I was being tested. But with Ana it was more about her helping me and vice versa. I was useful. Kaitlinn made it clear to me that I wasn't.

About time I made her rethink that.

Chapter 5 (Ana)

THE REST OF THE TROOPS walked off with Jacobs. I watched 'em head back, ready for another fight, and wondered if Dawn was right, that they'd just be picked off. They had a fighting chance if they got to a Storehouse. But there were also the roving bands. I half wondered if Jacobs was into more than he let on, if he had information about the Guard he didn't want shared with Dawn and the non-Action side of the Coalition.

Jacobs stopped and gave me a look as the others walked about him down the path toward the Storehouse. The serious glint in his eyes faded and his lips turned up a little. He arched his arms up in the Valkyrie salute, and I returned it. We watched each other for a moment, two ragged warriors more than ready to take a break from this endless trip around the outlands but unwilling for any surrender that wasn't part of our total victory. Much as guys like him could be pricks, I knew if things really got hot, he'd have taken a shot to the chest for me. I'd have done the same for him too.

We shared this thought without a word spoken between us. He turned around again and was gone.

Dawn led the way toward the Capital at first. I was a little amazed until I realized she was staring at her P-LAD for directions. I couldn't help but wonder if her intellect was limited to her technology access.

There we were, a Warrior, a Worker, and an Intellectual Product, a cross section of what Lebabolis represented in its essence. Three of us working together, but not how they had planned.

After Jacobs' outburst, Dawn claimed we had even less time than before. With Treg and me close behind, she hurried over the leaf coated ground. Her trail sent flurries of leaves around, and the branches in her way snapped back as if in surprise. I watched her relentless pace and chuckled to myself as I waited for a stumble from her. The warm air brushed past us with each step we took. The air was dank with the smell of leaves both growing and rotted.

Finally, she stumbled over an exposed root, but that only slowed her down for a second. It was like she was in a trance with just every so often making an adjustment. A slight turn here, a little jag there, but her pace was as steady as a Radomet. We pawed our way past the branches that flung back angrily in the path of Dawn's wake.

"Watch it!" Treg called out. "You may know the way, but we need to be careful."

"It's fine," she said. "I scanned this area; there are no traps." Her arms swung wide, with not even a glance back our way.

I wondered if my comment to Jacobs that she was on the up and up was gonna bite me on the ass. Treg shrugged and rolled his eyes at me as if he'd heard my worries out loud.

"Hear that, Treg? The Intellectual says there are no traps. Maybe she can get on her little play pretty there and fetch us a ride, save her precious little feet from all this abuse."

Dawn stopped short and darted back to us. As fast as she'd moved ahead, she rushed back within an arm's length from Treg and me. Her precious P-LAD was clutched tight to her side, and her deep blue eyes pierced into ours. She held her gaze on us; her only other motion was the excited heaves of her chest. Beads of sweat formed on her crinkled brow. She switched her glare between Treg and me. In her eyes was a blend of aggravation with some fear too. By sheer reflex, I felt my scowl deepen.

"You think I wanted this? You think I wanted to be out here with any of you people? I was perfectly happy where I was, in a lab doing research for Charista, when she pulled me out for this. I'm sorry that I don't see any reason to be here any longer than possible."

"We were happier when you weren't an appendage to us, too," I said speaking for both Treg and me.

"You made the deal, you live with it. Just like me."

I gave serious thought to ripping the device out of her hand and popping her with it. The tightness in my gut spread to the rest of my body and I could feel my teeth clench. I'm not sure how I managed to speak instead of whack her, but I did. "So you want to get back to your little death facility, I get that. Until then, you're not under the cozy umbrella of the Capital out here. We're a team, get it? So you best listen up to the people who've covered combat areas on foot more than you."

"How about you show me some courtesy as well?"

"How about you give me more than two feet of space," I said, raising my weapon up to my chest, and in a flat tone I whispered, "How about it?"

That's when Treg stepped in between us. She shook her head and glanced at her P-LAD until he grabbed her shoulder. "See, we don't get to play with just our own Product here. It's all about one in the Action—excuse me—the Coalition. And that means what's best for every... one. Get it?"

It was my turn to pull him back as Dawn blurted out, "You weren't so successful you didn't need to make a deal with Lebabolis, now, were you?"

For someone who was supposed to be smart, she didn't have an ounce of self-preservation.

What she did have was luck because Treg and I both felt like she wasn't worth the trouble of killing.

Treg shouldered his rifle. "Call out directions from the rear, and let us with the guns do what we do."

Dawn tapped her P-LAD in thought. "I guess you have a point." She averted her eyes and pointed in the way she'd been headed when we'd stopped. I felt a tinge of relief at what was the most progress we'd made yet on this hike.

"I'll cover the rear." When Dawn eyed me, her eyebrow arched. I added, "Don't worry, honey, I'll have his back, and I just might cover yours too."

Treg flashed me a wink and activated his rifle as he stepped out ahead. Dawn followed in the middle, and I held the rear up. We were as prepared for action as anyone could've been in our situation. My hand found the handle of my dagger. I'd be able to toss it at somebody if needed. It sure came in handy on the Verge back to 2014.

I smirked to myself thinking back to when Jacobs had his gun at her chest. He'd have blasted her wide open, and then we'd be off somewhere else. But I couldn't do that. I had a deal and I had to focus. If nothing else, for Varrick. What would become of him if I didn't?

Dawn's eyes slid to Treg then back to me every so often. She wasn't sure she could trust us, but she finally realized she didn't have a choice. Our pace was slower this time as she pointed out dips and breaks in the ground ahead.

My gut eased a tad when it looked like we had made a breakthrough with her. However, the searing hunger pains I'd felt back in the crater were creeping in much worse by now. While the thought of food was appealing, the idea of what we had to go through to get it wasn't. I took a few deep breaths and focused on ignoring the nag of my belly. I looked through the woods every chance I got but saw nothing even close to being food.

The outskirts of Lebabolis, where we were, were barren. Any worthwhile food was harvested from this place a long time ago. A person could find food if they had some know-how and some time, but we were short on both.

"Can't you find a Verge on that P-LAD of yours and get us through this quicker?"

"Not since the Omegans started using Darkness and made the Verges unstable."

We walked on in silence for an hour. The forest provided just enough sound that covered up the noise of our breaths. The periodic chirp of a bird and the smooth rustling of leaves were the only noise for a while, until my curiosity got the better of me. I thought of how wide the Coalition was, and the fact they had stuck me with Dawn, of all people. An Intellectual Product. Ok, she could've helped when it came time to work with Cataclysm, but why now? We were in a bad way out here, and another Warrior Product would've been far better.

My boredom had gotten as bad as my hunger. "So laboratory, huh. What were you making in there, more Radomets?"

Dawn glanced over her shoulder but kept walking before she said, "Not quite."

"Well, what then?"

"Chemical experiments." Her answer was squeezed out as easy as someone who'd been tortured for it.

"So then, Radomet research."

"No, not that. We were studying the effect of a new virus on humans."

That stopped me short.

A jolt of disgust hit me like a fist to the midsection. Visions of Varrick and the others with Pox flooded my head, and along with my progressing hunger it made me dizzy.

A new virus?

I knew they'd already experimented on augmentation like with Radomet, but this was the first I'd heard about there being biological weapons in their programs. "You're telling me you developed biological weapons for use on people?"

"For defense purposes."

"Defense from what?"

"Oh come on, Ana. You know about the groups out in the Outlands. You don't remember, or perhaps you were too young, but we had raids in the city. Why else do you think we made such a well-trained army?"

"OK, got me there. What kind of virus?"

"Is this really important right now?" She flashed a worried look.

"Maybe, maybe not. Ya know, you can call 'em experiments

when they're in a lab, not when they are used on real people. And Dawn, when you toss me that scared look, it makes me wonder what else you're up to and why you're really here."

"What do you mean?"

"I bet you heard by now a lot of our people came down with this thing we call Pox. It's lethal, and so far no one's been able to treat it. My little brother has it, and Charista promised she'd cure him and our people. Seems a little strange to me if she'd make that claim and not have some kind of person like yourself to back that up."

"That would be strange alright."

The heat of the woods I'd been sweating off just coursed through me, but this time it was anger. It could've been the shakiness in her voice, or the weeks and months of running ragged with little to no sleep or food, or just the damn stupid smirk on her face right then, but a switch flipped in my head. Everything at that moment had to wait for me to set her straight. The Capital, the Valentium; even Cataclysm and Varrick had to wait for me to take care of this.

I grabbed her shoulder and spun her back until our eyes were directly across from each other.

Treg approached us. "What's going on?"

"A little girl talk, Treg."

My face seared, but the warm air had nothing to do with it. My gaze dug into her eyes like a needle. Dawn panted, her eyes wide. "W-what are you—"

"I'm not too happy about this either, but since you never bothered to ask Treg or me how we felt about being stuck with some low-life Lebabolis scum, I'll just say it. It sounds like you're avoiding telling me something, and I'm not too good with secrets. So I'll ask you one question, nice and easy, and you better tell me straight or you'll regret it, I promise."

"O-OK."

"Did you develop Pox?"

Multiple beads of sweat formed and trickled off her forehead. Her eyes looked in several directions before they returned to me. "What do you mean?"

"It's not a complicated question. An Intellectual Product can handle it. Did you develop Pox?"

"Does it make any difference now? Your brother, your people have—"

And she was avoiding again. Time for more persuasion. In a breath, the dagger was in my hand and at her face. She squealed at the cool blade pressed into her flesh. A tear joined the sweat that now poured off her face.

Treg gripped my arm, but I flung my shoulder and broke his grip.

"Ana, what are you—"

I held my hand up and waited for Dawn's response.

Her eyes were wide and focused on the blade an inch away from her right one. "OK, yes, yes, yes I did. But I was part of a team. I wasn't alone."

"Same difference. Doesn't make you any less guilty. Like when you blew our craft up."

"That wasn't me!"

Her eyes still hadn't convinced me. "I'm watching you, twitchy. I get any, and I do mean any, funny feelings about you, I'm knocking your ass out and dragging you to the Capital. I've been wound up for a while, and I think the exercise would do me some good."

At that moment I prayed there was a Verge nearby that I could've jumped back through so I could've eliminated every person who had developed that illness, including Dawn. But there was nothing I could do. We were stuck, and so was she. The emptiness of my options made me even angrier, and I was back to thoughts of what I'd do to Dawn to relieve some of this.

Treg squeezed my arm that held the blade. "There's no time, and you know we need her. Let's go."

I gave her another moment to wonder how far I'd take this, then pulled back and walked on with Treg. Dawn followed behind us at a safe distance.

"The hell's with you?" Treg asked.

I shrugged. "She's bugged me. For a while now."

"She's up your ass by assignment. Of course she'd bug you.

Can't you just deal with it?"

"It's kinda tough when she's one of those who made my brother and the rest of our people sick. You know, people in the Action? Dammit Treg, they poisoned us. Why don't you care?"

Treg crouched under a low branch. "Hey, you know I do. But we made this play with them. We got a deal, and you heard Charista. She'll cure them if we finish it."

"If she can."

"Now we know for sure they developed Pox, so they can also stop it."

I glanced back at Dawn, several steps back. Her eyes widened when they met mine. I took a little satisfaction from her apprehensive stare as I turned back around slowly to continue our trek.

We walked in silence for another hour. The path got rougher, and each time I lifted my feet over a fallen branch or stump my hips rewarded me with shooting pains. My stomach ache had progressed into a mild burning sensation by then. I strained to think of when my last actual food was. A week? Could it have been that long?

"Treg, how bout a break, huh? This walking is killing me."

"Can't keep up with the Warriors, Worker Product?"

I tossed a branch at him. "You know better. Come on, let's rest for a few."

Dawn was surprisingly agreeable about stopping. Amazing how a blade to a person's face can change their whole disposition. We pulled up against a cluster of trees and lay back on the grass. The light from the sun dotted the leaves and ground around us and made jagged shadows on the ground of our surrounding foliage. Dawn leaned on a tree off to one side of the clearing on the far end away from us. I drank the rest of my water, which amounted to two gulps. It wasn't even enough to soothe the itchy dryness that stretched down my throat.

Treg sat across from me, his legs crossed and rifle leaned over his shoulders. His eyes scoured the land around us, but like I'd seen, there was nothing.

"Treg, we need rations. Anything. What Sector are we

closest to?"

He sighed. "No clue. Better ask Dawn; she's got the nav data."

"Do I have to?"

"Wherever we are is the outskirts of Lebabolis. They trained us in spots like these, but I wasn't in this exact one."

Dawn alternated between gazes at her P-LAD, cautious looks our way and around the woods as if she could find some food and prove us both wrong. She'd be the hero Intellectual Product who got one over on the Warrior Product and warrior type who couldn't fend for themselves in the wilderness.

"Think it's a good idea we talk, based on our last conversation?" The thought made me chuckle.

Treg watched Dawn for a second, then replied, "Just be less you, and that'll be a start."

I kicked a patch of leaves into Treg's lap in response and approached Dawn. She held her water bottle up, so the scant drops in it fell into her mouth as I neared her.

"Hey."

She pulled the bottle back and jerked her head in my direction.

"We need food and water soon."

She resumed her gaze around the woods. "How about we find a stream?" Dawn looked at her P-LAD and checked the maps.

"I got another idea. Let's try a housing unit in the nearest Sector."

"That wouldn't be smart," Dawn said, avoiding my stare.

"Try necessary. Where are we; what Sector's close?"

"You realize the Omegans were spotted in groups in most Sectors?"

"I'm not saying we mount a damned offensive. We peg the housing units, we pop in, grab some rations, pop back out. We need a recharge. It's at least another half day to the Capital, right?"

"We should keep going; we've had enough delays."

"But we might have to detour again, and the Capital isn't expecting us. What if it takes a while to get through to 'em? And what if the Omegans are there too? We may have to hide

64

and wait longer than we think or draw down on a bigger force. In either case, we should be ready to wait longer than we think."

She looked down toward the P-LAD in thought. I looked at the screen for any hint of a tracker or a link to Charista. I was waiting, hoping to see anything that would've justified what Jacobs thought and given me a green light to tear into her. But nothing except her eyes locked on mine. "You're not going without me."

"As if I didn't know that." I smirked. "Get the coordinates and we'll make it happen."

Dawn's P-LAD screen flashed into nav mode and scrolled several maps as well as our location before it displayed a jagged red line between two sites. "We're near the border between Sector Two and One. We could arrive at a housing unit, maybe 15 or 20 minutes from here."

"That sounds good." I motioned Treg over and pointed toward Dawn's P-LAD. "So according to Dawn there's several housing units nearby. We gotta be light and quick about it; you know the Omegans are in a lot of places, and the ones who aren't trying to get to the Capital are busy scouring the rest of Lebabolis for anyone who didn't make it to the Capital for Lockdown."

"If we come up against more than five of them at once, it's not gonna be pretty... for us."

"I know. There's foraging around here, but I haven't seen anything edible since we started. Besides, there could be snares set out here. I'm sorry, but I'm not trusting what's in her little P-LAD scan here. We rely too much on that tech, and it's gonna get us killed one day. Besides, the Omegans are just as interested in pilfering the housing units as we are, so they won't rig 'em."

Charista started the Lockdown not long after the fight in Sector Five as a precaution. According to what Charista said, all Products were brought to the Capital with little to no notice. It was a little like how I left in Exodus, but this time in broad daylight. People took whatever they could get together in that short of time. My gut screamed at me that there had to be some supplies left behind. Then again maybe my gut just yammered for a meal. In any case, it was our best chance for getting food and any info besides the secret alerts Dawn chose to share with us. I was hopeful for some weapons, but the reality was we may just score a bit of food someone had no time to carry.

"Why don't we make this detour even more worthwhile and look for a Storehouse too?" Treg asked. "Would be nice having more firepower for the rest of this trip."

"Can we locate 'em?"

"Warriors were shown the ones for their sectors, but that's about it. And this isn't where I grew up." He fluttered his lips and looked at me with a downtrodden gaze.

Treg set his rifle down and folded his arms behind his back. "Before we jump on this, what about the Valentium? They'll be around for that too, and I don't want to hit on any pockets of that stuff they just happen to have a unit guarding or anything. It'll be bad enough if we hit a roving patrol, but they'll be jacked up at the Valentium sites; they'd waste us in a blink."

"No deposits in the immediate area," Dawn said as she looked back at her P-LAD. "There's always potential they exist but don't show up on this device. I think it's worth this already risky idea."

Treg nodded me over to the side. We walked several feet away, out of earshot from Dawn.

"You think we can trust her? A minute ago you were about to fillet her throat and now we're trusting her to find us food?"

"I hate to be going off my gut right now so much, but it's all I got. I figure she's out here like us. And I gotta think, if she's that concerned with not leaving my side, she wouldn't put us or herself in a situation that would jeopardize it."

"She's gotta be hungry, like us?"

"Yeah, but she also wants to get back to her people, like us to ours. So we help her, and ourselves. It sucks, but it's the Coalition."

"Helluva motto." He nudged me.

Dawn had returned to her P-LAD. I wondered if she just had maps on it still, our nav path, or if she'd relayed some update back to Charista, our coordinates for something else. I looked forward to the time when we'd be free of her and no longer need to be under this deal that felt like anything but one.

Chapter 6 (Nelson)

THREE LOUD BLASTS thumped me in the chest, and I gasped for air.

People around me looked at each other and me as if to ask if everyone else had felt the same thing just then. I checked the skies for any incoming craft around, but there were none. Kaitlinn passed a glance over the scene, her arched eyebrows melded into a scowl that pierced the area in a sweeping arc like a lighthouse beam until her eyes fixed on one spot. She muttered, "Damn."

The temporary facilities belched black smoke into the air. Soldiers rushed in and around the vehicles. Some checked what had happened, others rushed to help people injured in the blasts. The explosion hadn't affected the Hell Hawks for the moment, but crews near the ships stopped their repairs and fired up their engines, and sent the ships further away from the spreading flames.

Some spots burst into flames that lapped at people nearest them. Kaitlinn swung the P-LAD about, and she looked like she wanted to fling it toward the facilities in frustration.

"We've got a problem," Kaitlinn said it to no one in particular, and without any hint she caught the irony of us having a single problem amid a sea of nine million other catastrophes. I felt right then like I was a director of some weird documentary about a military commander with virtually no knowledge of their situation who made their best attempt at control out of chaos.

Kaitlinn tapped madly on her P-LAD. Diagrams flashed back and forth, and readout flickered like a strobe light. She scratched her head at some schematics which flashed over the screen very quickly.

Kaitlinn let out a deep sigh. "Kado worked on this problem ever since the Coalition was even formed. I thought we had more time before this happened."

"Before what happened?"

"These units were meant for Valentium exploration and mining, and nowhere near the level of abuse they've been getting. We're pressing them too hard."

"So what then?"

She fixed her eyes back on her P-LAD, with no acknowledgment I was even there. "Baudricort was smart, using them in his Exodus. They're the only way to move so many people out very fast. But even he'd admit this trip to the Range is a long shot. We'll get them moving somehow. There's too many people to handle otherwise."

She nodded in agreement with her own idea. I wondered just how many would've gone along with the likelihood of that. She scanned the area again until her eyes met mine and a name popped into my head. It was in part wishful thinking, but now more than ever it looked like she needed him too.

"Can Kado help us out?"

She gazed down at her P-LAD, as if the answer was already there. Maybe it was. Just then I was hit with an odd regret for the times I'd spent with my eyes glued to a smartphone or other device screen while in conversation with someone. Weird how that little nugget of perspective popped up at me right then.

"Our priority is security and defense; we can't have one without the other. It's too risky, shuttling him back and forth. No, he's safer where he is. I've got a unit guarding him. Both of you are important, too important to chance being out in the open, unprotected."

"Me continuing to, you know, breathe is pretty important to me."

She took a slow breath, her eyes pierced into me. "No, it's too dangerous. If need be, we can relay information to him on a comm."

"How about a deal?" I asked.

"Mr. Forrester, I thought I made it clear, I won't risk you out in the open like that. There's a place for you, and right now that's within my sight. If you want to be of use, keep people away from the flames."

My eyes fell to her P-LAD as she continued her argument. I saw a map of the area, and just then, a tight ball of tension built in my stomach, but I realized it was another Pull. This one was a little like the feeling I had when I saw the map with Baudricort and Ana, and located Cataclysm. Only this time, the display jumped more, and it had nothing to do with her hand.

There on the map, an overlay of icons appeared, like some kind of strange computer program. And I just knew the icons were us, the Coalition. One icon slid across the map and then several more markings of a different shape appeared. Above this the text "Omegan attack in 12 hours" in bold red letters framed the image up.

And then the air around me went into a haze and I saw more explosions. Like before, when I saw Ana in the woods, but this time I was in an open field during a battle. I felt the hot wind from ships that swooshed by above, the thundering ground from troops rushing about, Coalition and Omegans. Then there was the hot singe of pulse fire that rocketed past almost too close to avoid.

I saw Kaitlinn as she fell to the ground, and blood trickled from her mouth. Ana flashed into view too; she had a knife poised at her throat. My fear had me frozen. It was all I could do just to keep my eyes open. An Omegan attack? Was this the future? Trouble about to happen?

I heard warbled speaking and then a click. The visions faded back to the burning facilities and where I had been a moment earlier. I looked back at Kaitlinn, who held her gaze on me.

"Well, what do you have to say about that?"

"I'm sorry?"

"I asked, if you're supposed to be this prophet Xander, what should we do here?"

I chewed my lip and watched her, then looked back to the map. Just like that, this field commander of the Coalition, a decorated soldier of Lebabolis, asked for my strategic assessment. I felt like I'd just been given four kings in a hand of poker and it was time to call.

"What if I told you I knew where and when the next Omegan attack is happening?"

Her eyebrow arched. "I'd say tell me where."

"Nah uh. You know what I want."

"Oh?"

"Get me Kado, either here or there."

"Did you forget the part where I explained how dangerous that would be?"

"You need help, as do I."

"So you're holding out on me?"

"I'm bargaining. There's something wrong with this device he put on me. If you do that, or get him here, I'll tell you what I know. And you better do it before whatever this is I'm having gets worse."

Her jaw twitched. "Suppose I just yank it out of you?"

"Yeah, but you don't know that wouldn't kill me, huh? You willing to risk that?"

"I'm beginning to think it's worth a chance."

"I bet Ana would have a lot to say about that, not to mention Charista."

She inched closer to me until her breath tickled my nose. "So that's how it is?"

"Looks that way."

Her eyes reddened. They widened, and her scowl tore into me. I took several deep and noisy breaths, then swallowed the lump in my throat, but I felt my feet rock stead beneath me. She thrust the P-LAD to her side. Her eyes narrowed and her lips drew in a line. "Norg will bring him here. You'll stay with me. Is that clear?"

"Fair enough."

"No, answer the question. Is that clear?"

"Crystal."

"While we're tending to that, I'm giving Llewyn an update. He needs to know, in case his facilities start breaking down like ours. He needs to be ready if the Omegans slip past us and the rest before we can get mobile again. We're making good on our deal to protect the Action, like you are on Cataclysm."

"Alright."

"And you'll be there when I contact them so we'll both know what's going on in that brain of yours."

"Why not? Lots of people want inside my noodle these days. At least I know you want me for my mind."

#

Kaitlinn took me into a darkened room. Three chairs stood around a table with a comm in the center, a small disk shaped object. When Kaitlinn activated the comm, Llewyn materialized above the device, a disembodied head that wafted in midair in front of us with a bluish glow. She started the conversation and rattled a lot of details off from their facilities and much of it went over my head. She spoke words that melded into gobbledygook about system problems. At best I recognized every fifth word she said. But even being back home, a mechanical conversation would've glassed me over more than listening to a golf game on TV.

All I was good for in maintenance was driving my car in to Firestone when the little red light told me so. I had a great imagination for creating this world, but imagination is where it ended. I refocused on her assessment when she got back to regular English.

"It's pretty bad. The units are having multiple issues. Ultra-hydraulics, drive systems, general maintenance problems. These units aren't holding up to all this traveling. We both knew this would happen at some point, I just hoped it would've been

72

closer to the Range."

Llewyn squinted in thought. "So what then? How do we fix this so we can keep going?"

"It'll take a lot more than elbow grease and wrenches." Kaitlinn sighed.

I leaned toward the comm as she spoke. "Look, while we're discussing options, why don't we just make a grab for Cataclysm? It's out there, and Charista's hell bent on finding it any way she can."

Kaitlinn eyed me. "Ana and Dawn are part of the deal."

I gazed into Kaitlinn's eyes in the hope that maybe I'd gotten a breakthrough from her and she'd for once listen to one of my suggestions. Instead, I got a face I'd have expected from my old high school disciplinarian. Kaitlinn's brow was creased, and her face was littered with sweat, some grime and an expression sour even by her standards. "You don't realize what you're dealing with there. Charista is adamant Dawn is to be part of the retrieval. I can't allow you to go on your own."

I figured on another approach and decided I'd flex my snark muscle. "Kaitlinn, are you afraid of not doing something Charista tells you?"

"That's none of your damned business. I'm more concerned with our people. Cataclysm is Ana's job."

"Right, but who's to say where Ana even is right now? We're not sure she's still alive." My throat tightened when I said that last part. Thinking that idea for a second, her not being around anymore, scared the hell out of me. As much as I'd been through in all of this, she was the one constant that kept me going. And my thoughts of getting home took on new life once I saw what she went through and was still going through for me. She taught me that the darkness out there was nothing I couldn't overcome and break through like the sun piercing a thick cloud front. She never flinched, coming centuries back for me, even it if meant leaving her brother behind to an illness. Thinking of her tireless trip and continued surge filled me with energy and a sense of why I was here after all. If she made it across all those centuries to me, what was a trip of several hundred miles in comparison?

"What are you suggesting here?" Llewyn asked.

"I've got the P-LAD from the Valkyrie. It's got coordinates on it and some other text. It was encoded, and no one's been able to break that, not even Kado with his gear. But there's something he doesn't know, that none of you do either.

Kaitlinn and Llewyn's eyes were glued to me.

"I can read them."

They both cackled in response. Kaitlinn shook her head. "Ridiculous. Now I'm wondering if the time displacement sickness hasn't induced delusion in you. Perhaps you really do need an examination from Kado."

I then reached for her P-LAD, which she slid just out of my grasp. "Show me the maps for the Range."

She pulled up the diagram, and with the Link open to Llewyn I sat back and breathed deep. I was getting better at controlling the Pull when I wanted to. It was happening on demand, even deeper than I'd felt before. A tremor rippled through me at first. My throat seized for a few seconds, then I felt a trail of heat spread from my mouth down into my stomach. I took several quick breaths before I rattled off a litany of words, many of which I had no idea about. They sounded like coordinates and the Greek language. Did I know Greek? I took a class, but that was ten years ago. Back then I only knew things like how to describe my dog after he had a drink of water. What I was babbling could've been words similar to what Kaitlinn had rattled off a few minutes before. For me, it wasn't a matter of comprehension, but more like regurgitation. It was as if I had an MP3 player in my brain and someone had just pressed play on the most bizarre playlist ever. Kaitlinn's gaze faded from a cynical grin to mild amusement to downright shock.

I rattled off names and locations of not just the Range, but of other areas near it. I spoke names I'd never heard, in pronunciations I had no clue I'd known. My mind and mouth became like a water pump that spurted information out. Had I not seen the look on Kaitlinn's face, her mouth wide open in amazement, I would've happily accepted a strait jacket and an all-expense paid trip with accommodations in a padded cell.

I handed her P-LAD back and swiped my hand through my hair. "I never said anything when I first found out. Baudricort tried to jam me up to the Link and pull it out of me, and I was afraid what he might have done if I told him about this. But yeah, I can read it. The words just form into where I can read them, like magic."

"So we've got the source of this code, but not the means to get to the Range any faster. The Omegans are around, and sooner or later we'll be in the thick of this again no matter where we go."

"Can we get anyone there, Kaitlinn? It's worth a hit to your numbers if we can get Cataclysm."

"All I need is a transport and one other person." I smirked when I thought of just who I wanted. I knew if there was anyone I had a fighting chance of staying alive with, it was him.

"Give me Norg and I'll go. I'll find it."

Kaitlinn shook her head. "We must reposition first. We've got an edge if we know where Cataclysm is, but right here we're far too vulnerable, this many troops and vehicles in one spot. Besides, I won't chance us getting to Cataclysm first with two people only to have you captured or killed by the nearest Omegan group that happens along. Once this regiment is better dispersed, I'll spare a detachment for you. In the meantime, we'll get word via comm from Kado on a temporary solution to this problem so we can get going again. Once we handle the facility issue, you and a detachment take off ASAP, head straight for the Range and that location. Meanwhile, keep your comms open and report back on the first thing you see or if there's trouble, you got that?"

I released an anxious sigh. "Yeah."

Chapter 7 (Ana)

THANKS TO DAWN'S P-LAD coordinates, we threaded ourselves through very thick brush and made it into the cleared outskirts of Sector Two. The gentle stillness of the woods was fast replaced with vacuum silence, the stale sound of nothing. It was like someone paused the sector in its tracks. The emptiness in the air made me queasy. The woods were a sea of noise compared to this.

Even knowing about the Lock Down protocol, the empty streets and buildings that greeted us felt very weird. Everything was vacant. Vehicle paths were littered with shards of clothing and rations containers, signs of a mad scramble. Tire treads from where trucks pulled people and drove them away from here snaked along the pathways headed out of the sector. The signs that normally displayed work assignments were smashed, and instead spat sparks out in a regular tempo like an electric fountain. The functional boards displayed the standard Lockdown message.

Rule one in a Lockdown was you made it to the Destination any way you could. The regular transports weren't there, of course. The whole place looked like a fake construction site, a decoy Sector. The only noise I heard was the low whine of the evac alarms while we walked around.

My gut drew taut when I felt my boot crunch over a busted P-

LAD on the ground. The droning alert was the only sound around us. This weird feeling settled on me like a moth. My arms tightened, and my mind went to that place it did when there was trouble. I learned this from Treg—if you lose your bearings for too long, you become a target.

Focus. Center yourself on the immediate area.

The problem was the immediate area bugged me more than anything.

I looked around at the housing units, ten alone on the path we walked. Any decent sniper set up on top one of those buildings could've gotten a shot off at all three of us. I watched Dawn and hated to admit it, but for at least this part of the trip she was right. We had let our hunger call this move. I had a bad feeling it was gonna bite us back hard. If the Omegans or anyone else wanted to, we would've been easy pickings for even their worst soldiers.

I peered around while Treg stepped ahead of us, his rifle aimed forward. I wondered about the people who lived in these units and what had happened to 'em. Did they make it? Not too long ago I was one of 'em. In a dangerous event, we'd be ushered to a safe place. We had practiced for things like Valentium Core reactor meltdowns, but I had never seen a real evacuation by Lebabolis.

It impressed me how everyone looked to be gone; I hoped all of 'em made it to the Capital for lockdown. Of course, all Lebabolis had to do was dangle the promise of food and they'd be off. Those were the reins: food, work, purpose, ingrained through the Link. For those who accepted it anyway, acceptance meant more like absorption. They kept every product working and humming along like a well-tuned machine. Aside from the Deviants in Custody, the rest of their Products got on well with the program. The Deviants were eventually turned into Drone Products, or Radomet if they had enough physical potential.

Most Products were so lulled and guided by the direction of having work to do—the same work day in and day out—they didn't need much to have to pull up and get to the Capital any way possible. Most of 'em would've crawled there if they had to.

That's why the Exodus was still the best idea for a lot of people, even with Baudricort's absence. There wasn't time to organize it better. They just had to get as many to safety and let the sorting work itself out later, once we decided just what and who we'd be. In this system I was more warrior, but maybe there'd be another choice—farming, or even leader? What if those choices included a family of my own? A chill ran up my back at the idea I could be someone other than who I was right then.

I'd never been through a real lockdown, but the complete emptiness of everything around us just felt strange, even wrong. I noticed scarring on some buildings and wondered if the Omegans picked off some stragglers during the move for Lockdown. But even so, if they did, where were the bodies? They wouldn't have bothered with clearing the dead away.

Or would they?

After a few minutes, my breaths slowed, and with the slight relaxing went the knotty soreness in my body. I was glad for once, being away from the fight, even if it was here. I walked further and glanced around at the peacefulness of this place. Trees were scattered around between the facilities, and small patches of grass showed some jagged darkened lines that looked like hurried steps of people in flight. The area almost looked lonely, like an abandoned animal that waited in sad silence for its owner's return.

I had time to breathe and adjust to what was going on for a change, and adjusting to people's plans weren't easy, especially Charista's. All of her moves since the Coalition were tough to figure, but so far I hadn't felt like she wanted to kill me. The Omegans were still enough of a threat, and her people, like Dawn, were here with us. I had enough value in Cataclysm alone. Problem was, what happened after I delivered it? Nelson and I had worth until then, but she wanted me to go after Cataclysm more than any of her people. There was some kind of weird trust between us, I guess.

I realized I hadn't heard that voice I'd heard at the crash site. I wondered if it knew about Baudricort and my mother. I still had so many questions, and I only felt more deep in this fog than ever. I wondered about how that bomb had killed Baudricort just moments after we'd seen him. I thought about maybe that was meant for Nelson or even me. My mind flipped through scores of faces and names, a sea of suspicion, but that's the sick and twisted game I played in my head. Like my father before me, I'd never stopped planning and working out my options. I figured as long as I kept at that, I had a chance at finding my way outta this mess and even getting Nelson back to his home.

A sharp ray of sunlight bounced off one of the windows and into my face. I winced and blinked to clear my sight of the glowing remnants in my vision. We had a play with Cataclysm, as long as we got to it first. With the mix of people in the Coalition, I was even less sure about who Nelson was left with. So help me, if I found out he was dead, whoever was responsible was gonna deal with me. I let that thought of his death linger a second, but just like earlier, I pushed it aside. I had to keep all the energy I had directed toward our next goal as much as possible.

Dawn observed her P-LAD, and I noticed some updates from Kaitlinn from over her shoulder. If Nelson was safe, he'd be with her. It was the smartest place, other than with me. Kaitlinn was Charista's top officer, and as much as Charista considered Nelson valuable, he'd be held under Kaitlinn's boot at all costs. Kaitlinn was a warrior though, and warriors aren't babysitters.

I wondered how Nelson dealt with being under constant watch from someone other than me. I mused if he'd handled it any better than I'd been with Dawn. Maybe Kaitlinn would've been easier; at least busier so she couldn't have been as close by as Dawn had been with me.

I hoped Nelson hadn't taken off on another rogue trip; there was no way I'd have known when or where to look out for him if he did.

My biggest problem was even if we delivered Cataclysm to Charista, there had to be a way out for us. We needed some kind of assurance before we delivered that kind of power to anyone.

Once she used it on the Omegans, then what? Was she serious on her promise to let us go in peace? I missed Baudricort a lot more at times like this, when my brain churned in overdrive with so many scenarios and options. I strained my mind to consider what he'd do in this situation.

And then there was the "Valkyrie" business.

It started not long after we repelled the attack at Sector Five and I faced down Commander Chun. Charista made her grand show, where she announced the victory to citizens on MODOSNet and took her credit for it. But people who were there and put out the fires and buried the dead and brushed the blood, dirt, and guts off their hands by my side knew differently.

They saluted me.

It felt weird, but by reflex I returned it, my hands crossed above my head, and mirrored them. I felt pain from not knowing what to tell these people. I wasn't sure where this Coalition was going, beyond the Range anyway. Wasn't that something a leader was supposed to know? All I knew was if I pressed ahead, I wouldn't be stuck. I had people's attention, but I also had no clue on this, and felt nothing like how I figured a leader felt. A leader handles their people, makes the tough calls and leads their group to win wars. Attacking a position, leading a charge, that was more me. I'd been shown that. But this path wasn't clear cut. I dealt with people who wanted more power and to keep theirs. The straight forward fight was my zone.

I was proud of the Action and that I stood with 'em, but that Valkyrie name bugged me. When I heard it from people in the Action or the Coalition, I felt like it was meant for someone behind me. There were looks too: the beaming eyes, the gazes of respect. They made me uncomfortable, but they continued. I brushed the hopeful glances of awe off best I could. Someone could refer to me as Valkyrie, but I'd never have called myself that. People said it to me like it was for a dignitary, but for me, it felt like a criminal sentence. Besides, the Valkyrie was always declared by the Coursons, the governing body of Lebabolis. They determined the strongest, bravest of their Warrior Products.

As far as I was concerned, that was ancient history, like they were talking about someone in an ancient book from one of those caches. I didn't like being told I was anything. I was somebody who had enough, that's it. Enough of being a part of a machine that only cared I was well enough to work for them. That didn't deserve a title. If it did, then how about Clara, the little girl who survived an attack on her whole Encampment by herself? The title, directed to me, felt odd, like a bulky costume I couldn't wait to take off.

Dawn's P-LAD chimed with an alert. A swirl of holograms appeared above it and there was Kaitlinn, reading a report. Kaitlinn reported she'd secured a Valentium point for fueling. That meant they had a group of people, and I bet some from the Circle were there. Most likely Norg and Zengus, but this time helped by Lebabolis and Radomet too. Her update continued on about mechanical problems the mobile facilities had. Buildings were stalling, breaking down, even blowing up. My heart sunk when I thought about our people, out in the open on their way to the Range, and the thought of them stranded in the open with little to no protection. A pang of guilt hit me at the idea the ones we fought for to make it to the Range were stuck like that. If Jacobs made it back to 'em, he'd be able to help. We became more and more like lost animals who had to be rounded up. I hoped Jacobs and his group would get back. As long as they weren't spotted and overtaken, they'd be mixing it up in no time.

Nothing appeared about Nelson on these updates, which made me wonder even more how he was. I didn't have a comm to contact him.

The area around the housing units was empty and quiet, like the vehicle paths. Crates and other boxes were scattered around as if some windstorm had flung packages and scrambled them around the streets. The green area with grass was a complete mess, jagged patches ripped out by too many feet in a dash across to be evacuated. Treg pointed to the green areas and commented on the tracks and the type of panic that must've happened. The place was full of stories, panicked people, and judging by the black char marks on some buildings, Omegan pursuit.

I pointed the blackened areas on the buildings out to Treg. "You think the Omegans hit 'em during the evac?"

He only gave a concerned look in response.

We watched the scene, like it was a set of giant still images that we walked through.

Treg leaned close, his voice in a whisper. "I'm gettin bad vibes. Let's get some supplies and head back to the woods quick."

Dawn and I nodded our agreement. With Treg in the lead, we slipped inside the nearest Housing Unit, HS17. The main area of the building was in shambles. Chairs overturned, the monitors on walls flickered on the Lebabolis logo with a message about evacuation and the lock down protocol. Over in a corner stood four familiar metal containers for ration storage. We shared hopeful grins with each other, and I made my way over to them while Dawn and Treg canvassed the rest of the area for any other kind of information or weapons.

I looked in the food stores in the units one at a time. The first two were empty, but the third one had a few left over rations. I grabbed 'em and checked the fourth, but it was also empty. Dawn scampered about and tapped into the console to search records. Treg headed upstairs.

Dawn scanned her P-LAD for any updates regarding HS17. "The Lock Down alert came too quickly and if there was an ambush, that explains why they never cut power."

"Guess the Omegans didn't learn the rule they're supposed to allow a head start on running like hell," I muttered.

After several minutes we met back in the lobby. Treg found a few containers of water and more rations, but nothing else. We eyed each other's haul for a moment and he said, "Look at us, rooting for scraps."

"Some things never change." I shrugged and smirked.

Dawn shook her head and skirted around us for another check inside storage cases.

I shoved some ration packs into my bag and watched Dawn for a second. "We better get—"

The low hum made my gut seize. It was the first sound we'd heard other than those alarms, and it was pretty clear a vehicle was approaching. There, up the road, a dark shape in the distance caught my eye, and when I focused that way I saw a group of transports headed our way. I motioned to Treg and he watched it too. "Crap. Omegan Patrol."

"We shouldn't have come." Dawn hissed.

I ignored her glare and crouched low behind a desk unit by the front windows. I lifted my head enough for a glance toward the approaching convoy. "Maybe they're just passing through; let's hide and see."

Much as it would've been nice to throw down on 'em, we were way light on weapons and even lighter on people we'd need based on the size of the truck, unless our surprise was for our own suicide. We raced to the second floor of the housing unit and grabbed spots low near a bedroom window.

"Better pray they aren't scanning this place, or we're toast." Treg cradled his rifle close and propped himself up against the bedroom wall.

I checked my pulse pistol. It registered half charge, and that confused me. Jacobs had given me this one before we split up. I hadn't fired it yet, so why was it half charged? These guns were kept on the ship.

The hum of the vehicle got louder until it sounded like they were on the street next to us. The vehicle stopped and the engine died. Then a low murmur built as several Omegans got out. Some of 'em worked with a large case. A few mechanical whirs later and we heard two of 'em talking. The tall and lanky one spoke with a gruff voice. "Assur is crazy; this won't work."

The other was a lot shorter and stocky. He answered, "That's not up to us. We're supposed to test the device here, so no one around sees what it will do."

The warm air in the room was more noticeable the longer we were in there, and soon we pulled at our body armor pieces, shirts, anything to release some of the heat that was building up from everywhere. Maybe they didn't kill the power, or they just killed some, like for the comfort generators.

Six others pulled a large dolly, covered with a dirty cloth. It had a dome shape and even with the six of them they struggled hauling it around. The tall and short ones directed the crew until the dolly was set how they wanted.

The short one waved to the troops to uncover the item. "Let's get this over with quick."

A few drops of sweat rolled into my eyes. I blinked back the burning and lifted up on my knees toward the window for a better look. The vehicle they rode in was parked fifty feet away from the housing unit. Two Omegans stood in a clearing another twenty feet away. A group of twenty other soldiers with weapons fanned out in an arc around them. The tall Omegan in the middle set up a mechanism on a tripod.

"What the damn hell?" Treg muttered.

They backed away from the mechanism. It was three small spheres joined together on a vertical rod. The other Omegan with the device tapped a red colored control panel and the spheres started rotating. A deep magenta glow appeared and got brighter the faster the globes spun. A loud hum built from this, and soon our window shook.

I looked back to the two Omegans. One of them swiped the air with his hand, like it was some kind of signal. The other pointed a device at the tripod. A loud roar burst from the spinning sphere, and a ripple of magenta colored light shot out from all sides. Everything shook and we were knocked backward onto the floor.

Treg's and my rifles powered down. He flipped his around for a few seconds. "It's totally dead. That thing's gotta be Darkness."

Dawn peered at the device for a few seconds, her lips drawn into a grim line. "Disruptor."

There it was. The first one I'd seen, and the very thing that had been giving us the most problems yet. Treg never explained that kind of weapon to me in our sessions; there never was enough time. I figured he knew about it from Warrior Product training.

"So that's where Darkness comes from."

Dawn eyed us with a tired glance. "You got it. If you've got any bright ideas on how to stop one of them once they've been turned on, you'd get a lot of people like Harkson, Charista, Kaitlinn, and Jason wanting to talk with you."

"There must be something we can do."

"Blowing it the hell up before they turn it on is a great start, but that won't happen. You're too late and hurling rocks is all you have left now."

I eyed Dawn with mild disbelief. Seemed a little foreign to me to not engage.

Dawn gestured out the window. "That's an Omegan platoon, thirty troops easy, most if not all armed. Think you're busting down there with two non-working guns and a lot of dirty looks?"

"Have to admit, Ana, she's got a point here. We made a dumb move 'cause we were hungry. Let's not graduate to stupid while we're at it." Treg shrugged.

My hands clenched the grip of my useless rifle. "Well, we can ID it and describe it to the others to look for it. That's better than—"

The front door to the unit opened and shut, and we heard footsteps downstairs. I yanked Dawn into the closet and snapped my fingers to Treg. My voice dropped to a hoarse whisper. "They're checking after effects, see what else it hit."

"Or they scanned for sigs after all," Dawn muttered.

"Either way, we'll get a jump on 'em if they don't see us coming."

"Right, so we can piss them off even more before they kill us."

Treg clutched both of us and gave a 'Quiet' sign.

The closet was a little cooler than the room, but just by a few degrees. By the time my pulse had sped up enough though, it made the place even warmer than the room.

My heartbeat thumped in my throat as I planted my hands against the wall behind me. I had to admit, I didn't give it much thought when I slipped in here with 'em. But what the hell else was there? If we hadn't been hungry as all get out, I wouldn't have even suggested this detour.

One of them entered the room. Their footsteps plodded slowly around the room and stopped short. They reached down, and after a short pause they grasped Treg's rifle and held it up. My breath hitched and I eyed Treg in the dim light. Treg's eyes burned and his mouth twitched. But he kept quiet, beads of sweat on his forehead his only other response.

My heart rattled in my chest when our visitor bumped against the closet door. They worked on disassembling the weapon when their comm unit burst to life.

"Eben, report."

Eben fumbled for a few seconds, then the rifle clanged loudly on the floor. "Here. Found some tech that is now disabled. The test looks to be successful. Should we check for stragglers, see if this weapon has an owner nearby?"

The reply came quick. "Wonderful. No time for anything else; Assur needs us back at base for a report on the weapon test. Let's go."

My heart thumped in my throat. I imagined Eben punching a hole through the door or even a wall and yanking us out. Treg and I could've fought him off, but what about the firing squad of a unit outside?

Chapter 8 (Nelson)

NORG WASN'T TOO FAR away, thank God, and made good on my idea to just go for Kado. I hadn't trusted Kaitlinn even before the call to Llewyn. I was done waiting for them to get a hold of things.

Norg and I hopped into a Landcrawler and hightailed it out of there. It felt good being on the road again, more in control of things, and unlike the last time I had protection the whole way. We drove for a few hours until we got to Kado at the test facility.

After our sudden breakout, the comm exploded with messages from Kaitlinn. Seems I was even more important to her than ever after that. She even broke off and followed us with a unit herself. I laughed at the thought of how much it pissed her off that we just went and did something not on her pre-appointed schedule. Of course, it didn't help our chances of staying hidden since she knew right where we were headed. We had a head start though, and that had to be good enough for the moment.

Kado was in a lab with Ashton, the Lebabolis regular who was there for the fight at Sector Five. Kado's hair was more messed up than usual, which really said a lot. He had the same frazzled look most in the Coalition had, but not many of us had his kind of mileage, with everything he kept running.

The lab was in disarray, and it amazed me that in spite of all the facility moves Kado still worked through plans for a new weapon. A pungent smell of burned circuits hung in the air.

Kado cradled a translucent circuit board like a father with a newborn baby. "We were lucky in Sector Five. The Omegans kept their big guns in the wings, and now it's our only hope that we somehow keep them from blowing us up."

"You mind telling me why Kaitlinn's so concerned with guns right now when these units are breaking?"

"They'll need them eventually; they'll have to stand and fight the Omegans at some point."

"I don't suppose in all your hopping around you heard anything about Ana?"

His head sank, a deep sigh escaped him. "No, and it's bugging me."

"I've got this feeling she's alright. I can't explain how—"

"That's not atypical for her. Look, she's a survivor. That much I know, and so do you. I'm one who looks for hard facts before any declaration, but I'm comfortable in that assessment for now. However, I'm more concerned about Cataclysm. Where does that mission stand?"

"Where? It's dead in the water, unless she got some miracle break that includes surviving a Hell Hawk crash."

"If Ana's around, she'll go for it. Dawn won't let her stop. I know Dawn. She's Charista's head of Tech and Research. I was surprised Charista let her out of the lab for anything."

"Can we trust Dawn?"

"No more than Charista. Cataclysm's worth the hunt, but you don't want it in anyone's hands who might abuse it."

Ashton adjusted controls on a console while Kado grabbed a device. It looked like a gun, but it was more slender than the pulse weapons I'd seen.

"We got the idea from the attack in Sector Five," Ashton explained. "I noticed the way their beams sliced into buildings and even our armor, and it gave me ideas on new approaches. I also used some of Baudricort's older notes, and here we go."

They traded places, Aston worked on the device with some tools while Kado talked to Norg and me. "It's our heaviest gun yet, power wise. It worked a lot better on the Omegan armor in tests; it'll give us more of an advantage against them."

"Fantastic," Norg remarked. "When do we field test?"

Ashton and Kado spoke a few quiet words with each other. Kado then mulled whatever they discussed and turned back to Norg. "We can test whenever."

Norg and I exchanged glances. He looked back to Kado. "How many of these ya got?"

"I've got 100 cloned up."

"That's it? Kaitlinn said we had enough for a regiment at least."

Kado clutched his head like a disparaged parent and winced as if Norg had just punched him. Which he had, only with words instead of fists. "Kaitlinn says a lot of things. Norg, in case you hadn't noticed, we're on the run right now."

"You don't know the half of it, Kado," I muttered.

"What?"

"She's coming here, or at least some of her people are."

"Now?"

"Yep. They aren't too far behind us. We aren't exactly here by her plans either."

"Yeah, well, we still need as many as we can get. In case you haven't heard, things ain't going too good for us right now." Norg slapped Kado's back.

Kado looked to me. "We'll do our best. So Nelson, what's the last you heard from Ana since the Crater?"

"Not a peep. We saw her ship crash. Kaitlinn tried raising the comms on her and that whole group with Jacobs, but nothing."

"Oh. Well, I'm sure they'll make contact as soon as they can." His eyes darted about. "She was with Jacobs? If anybody could've saved a ship, it's him. Trust me."

Kado gave Ashton and Norg a quick look before he said quietly to me, "I need to talk with you; stick around once this is over."

Kado handed the weapon to Norg, who clutched it like a boy handed his favorite toy on Christmas morning. "'Scuse me while we get acquainted."

As he headed out I blurted out, "Don't shoot your eye out, or you know, blow up the world."

While Ashton followed Norg outside, Kado motioned to the seat next to him.

"OK, first thing, you gotta check this device, man."

He glanced around my shoulder. "What's wrong?"

"I've been having these blackouts."

"Blackouts?"

"Yeah, I see people and places. I can't be sure, but they feel like they're from the future."

"You have the closest link to the timeline as anyone I've ever known, Nelson."

"Well, then there are the Pulls."

"What are those?"

"It feels like I'm being physically drawn toward Cataclysm."

"Does Kaitlinn know?"

"No."

"Good, better keep that quiet. I wouldn't even tell Norg or Ana." With that he sat me down and pawed at the device on my neck from the back. I felt nothing at first, just heard a few clicks and snaps. But then it hit me: a surge of pins and needles all over my body.

"Whoa, what the hell?"

"Sorry, Nelson. I should've warned you. This device releases a regular sedative dosage into your system. I just adjusted it to increase a little. Should stave the effects you've been describing."

"Stave, as in temporary?"

"Best I can do for now, I'm afraid. The key we're going for is so your mind doesn't lose its place on the timeline."

"So, like a bookmark?"

Kado slid back to my front. "Huh? Oh, those ancient paper tiles? Yes, I suppose. Now, I've got a few things to talk with you about before our visitor arrives." He pulled up his P-LAD and activated the holograph. A series of images floated by in a glowing blur.

"I was curious for the longest time why Charista was so

90

interested in you and Xander. She put so much effort into those Link messages, and even Baudricort went along in his own way, trying to have you send those messages, and then to have it come to nothing. I asked whoever I could. Otto didn't know anything and Baudricort was as evasive as he usually was."

On the screen appeared a huge crossed knife and bolt, the Valkyrie symbol. Kado stared at it before he turned to me. "Besides working on new weapons and coming up with fixes to the temporary facilities, doing what I can about the wounded and sick, I've done some digging of my own."

"Yeah? Anything good?"

"Plenty. Not sure if it meets your qualifications of 'good', but it's a start."

"Alright then."

"Yeah, I suppose. Kaitlinn and Charista are desperate for some kind of edge. It really concerns me that they don't have anything in their plans beyond finding Cataclysm though, and whatever tech we can conjure up here in the meanwhile. Anyway, in my digging, what I found really was inevitable, I suppose. In every project, enhancement, weapons research I went through, I came across some transmissions from Lebabolis."

"Transmissions?"

"That's correct. Some Link message artifacts, regular comms, random traffic. Reception's been spotty though. Lebabolis is sending information where they can via MODOSNet."

"Kaitlinn said it's broken."

"Damaged but not destroyed. If you know the system, you can find a way in. I did, but I also grabbed something else I didn't expect. I've monitored channels wide open, because we never know which ones will be used or tracked, and neither does Lebabolis. And one night there was something."

"You found something you weren't expecting?"

"Absolutely not." With that he tapped in a code and a group of documents appeared in the hologram. They had a lot of text on them, but my eyes went to the picture of Baudricort.

"I've been in Baudricort's upper group with Otto for a good

while. He was a good commander, but I always had this feeling he wasn't letting everything out to us. Otto and I talked about it. And right around when he started to share more details, and the maps to Cataclysm turned up, Baudricort ends up dead."

"Baudricort wanted the action to exist on its own, free from Lebabolis. We had people; we needed infrastructure. It was a long shot. But he figured the Range was our best play. At least basic shelter wasn't a concern there. This traipsing around in those portable buildings was never more than a temporary measure. Charista shrugged it off. But when the Omegans entered the picture again, she was suddenly interested in the Action."

"But why send Llewyn and those few to the Range? If there was that big a threat, why not all of Lebabolis?"

"That ivory fortress they have won't hold off the Omegans. She needs this weapon and us. She's not one to surrender either, but she'd consider a deal if it meant keeping her power."

"Lebabolis had us under their thumb. And so we broke free, Baudricort created the Action and we went with him because it was a chance for us. But instead, we ended up on the run from Charista, and as much as we fought her back and kept our move up, they still nipped at us until they once again had us—our sick were kidnapped. Ana wasn't the only one who was hit hard by those raids against our wounded."

"And now this." He grasped for the images in the air. They billowed around by his touch, as if it was a pool of water and he just jabbed his hand into it. He yanked his hand back and there with it was: a communication from Charista.

Agreement between Harkson Baronage, Chancellor of Lebabolis, and his eminence Zakmar of the Omegan Empire. Delivery of package in return for cease fire and immediate withdrawal of Omegan troops from Lebabolis soil. Arrangements for sharing Valentium to be determined at a later date.

Deal brokered by Charista Mantisword.

I froze on the words as if they were a hypnotic image and held me in a trance. I read them over again to make sure I hadn't imagined it. Nope, still the same.

"A cease fire? No, this isn't right. This isn't playing out like the story I wrote."

"Time's fluid, Nelson, remember. We make choices, we make mistakes, we triumph, we fall. All of it qualifies as adjustments. What we do today affects centuries down the line. Just you being here is unexpected."

"Well, we do have one thing in our advantage. I know where Cataclysm is."

"Yeah?"

"Close enough, anyway. When I looked at the Range maps, it came over me, like some kind of pull. I told Kaitlinn I'd help them find the next attacks by the Omegans."

"Does that really matter anymore? The attacks aren't going to matter a whole lot if she's got this deal and is part of it with Charista. I thought they were our escorts. They're more like a delivery service for the Omegans."

"Does Llewyn know about this?"

"He said no."

"You believe him?"

"I'm inclined to, given what this came from. The communications are garbled, Nelson. There's no way of knowing this wasn't some kind of false transmission to throw off anyone who could be trying to hack into our system, like the Omegans."

"Might be an attempt to draw us out, thinking there's a cease fire."

"They'd have been all over this on the comm by now if that was real, I have to think."

"Well, what is it then, some random transmission? And what's the package they mentioned?"

Kado's brow furrowed.

I scratched my head and thought about all the pieces at work. "It could be the Valentium. Norg told me when we left the crater how the Omegans switched from attacking us to harvesting all the Valentium they could carry. They pulled back from their attack for it even."

"So she's never really meant to cooperate with us, has she? She was just playing us and the Omegans until she got the deal she wanted? And now Llewyn's heading straight for a trap!"

"I'm more surprised that the Omegans were so willing to make a compromise. After all they've done, as strong as they've come on in fighting us and pushing us around, to just agree to a simple cease fire?"

"It doesn't make sense. We've got proof Omegans are in Lebabolis sectors, looting and roaming. That's not how two groups in a truce act toward each other."

Kado flipped through more records that detailed the terms of the cease fire. And the group to be exchanged was none other than the Coalition, headed right for the Range, where I was sure they were just going to be waiting for us.

"What about Kaitlinn; you think she knows?"

"If she does, Nelson, she's said nothing. I keep my head down because telling her anything is as good as telling Charista; you remember that. If she doesn't know, I'd just as soon cut my own throat than tell her. She's Lebabolis through and through. Hell, I bet she'll get some kind of citation and promotion for helping keep the rest of us in the dark."

"Could the deal be Cataclysm? Do the Omegans even know about it?"

"Can't say for sure. But they've got other tech at their disposal like a Disruptor, so they won't need a whole lot of firepower to get the better of us if our weapons are inert. It and the Valkyrie are what stopped them before, and I'm sure they won't forget that anytime soon. But I don't think they'd have any idea of where we've located."

"Could the Disruptor stop Cataclysm?"

"There's no way of knowing that before one's used against the other. It's never been tried; can't really say. I do know it's pretty damned volatile."

"Cataclysm?"

Kado's eyes bugged out, and for a second I thought he might grab me. "Of course, Cataclysm! Think about it, you've got Valentium, this already highly unstable substance. So much that it's bent the time continuum and allowed us to travel into the past and back. Now there's this weapon that at its core channels Valentium energy and can be directed to a focused location. It gave us a hell of a lot of power, but there was no guarantee that power wouldn't be contained. That's what the Valkyrie was referring to when she had it turned off and dismantled. Charista continually rejects the idea that what she's after could end up destroying us all."

"Disruptors weren't used when Cataclysm was last in play. All I know is one thing these Disruptors have done already is affect the Verge. And the Disruptors haven't been around that long to know what they are."

I felt a shudder and lurched back in my seat. The lights in the room dimmed, and I made out Kado's voice in the distance, as if I were underwater. "Nelson, you still with me?"

Lights flashed about me and the room spun. The twisting sped up until the walls liquefied and vanished. When it stopped the walls had faded into a forest. Several figures stood in the center and after a second my eyes locked on Ana, her knife poised at someone's neck. I couldn't see who it was, though I gazed directly into Ana's eyes. They were stark and wide, fixed with rage. Treg stood beside her and held Ana back slicing into the other person.

A rumbling sound broke that vision and then I was transported to the Range in a cave with Kado, Norg, and a group of soldiers. A device was off to our side, and I knew in my soul what it was.

Cataclysm.

We were on a rise, a jetty that extended out of a mountain. From a distance I saw a huge battalion of Omegan ships and troops. They converged on us with the ease and coordination of a python that slithered for an easy kill. Norg stood nearby and fired his rifle at the Omegans along with the rest of the troops. Then, I was whisked away over to one side of the field and saw another group. All of them had long mangy hair, and they wore torn outfits, or in some cases no shirts at all. They looked coarse, but their faces and eyes were as attuned as a panther perched to strike its prey. And at the front of this group, more disheveled than I'd seen her before but with eyes as animated as I'd ever seen and her face twisted in a battle cry, was Ana. With her in the lead, they barreled toward the Omegan forces. Just when they were about to collide, the sound of a thunderbolt popped me back, and there was Kado, his hand firm on my shoulder and a concerned look on his face.

"What happened to you?"

Beads of sweat cascaded about my face, and I huffed to catch my breath, but it was no use. Kado offered me a canteen, and more of the metallic sour water, but at that point it tasted like a mountain stream. I jammed my eyes shut and took a few slow gulps.

"Kado, it just happened again. I don't know why. Either it's got to do with me being here in the first place, or this device, or something else. But I'm seeing things, more than just the Pull to Cataclysm."

"What kind of things?"

"Places, people. Things I hadn't seen, and it makes me wonder if they're the future."

"What people are you seeing?"

"Usually they involve Ana. I see her with Treg, and just now saw her in the woods with someone, about to cut their throat."

"The device I gave you is a stabilizer. You are the only person who's been this far from his base time for this long. Your body was not meant to be displaced for this length of time. We found this out after we started making these Verge jumps and a few people came down with it. We called it time sickness. It went away not long after the person returned to their base time. But we've never had someone away for more than a week or two. You've been here more than a month now, right?"

"Yeah, that's right. I'm not telling Kaitlinn this, I'm still not sure about her either. But that deal over there is scary."

"I've seen some bad cases of time displacement sickness, Nelson."

"How bad is mine?"

He paused and checked notes. "Pretty damned bad. Look, we can't wait for Kaitlinn to be ready for strategy. She's got her own battles to fight. We also can't wait for Ana; she may not even be able to make a run. We need to take care of this."

"I can't go with you, Nelson."

"What, why? Come on, we may still have a chance to leave now. They aren't here yet."

"You don't understand. She's got a tracker on me. If I leave an assigned area, she'll know. I'll only be a liability for you."

"I don't think we should wait any longer for them to arrange the trip to the Range," I said.

"I wouldn't disagree. But Kaitlinn won't provide support. If you and I break for Cataclysm on this, we're on our own, and she won't let you slip away that easily."

"I wouldn't think she would. But if we had some extra help, like Norg, we could make a better run for it. Think you could get some kind of comm up to Ana in the meanwhile? She should know about this deal."

"It's dicey at best."

"She's alive, I'm sure of it. I can feel it."

Kado smiled. "Much as she's been through, I'm sure you're right on that. Even if Treg got zapped along the way, I feel bad for the person tries to take her down."

"But your tracker, maybe we can disable it?"

"She hooked it to the Link. New tech."

"I thought that was shut down."

"The old one was, but this is tech that came online outside of that. Bloodborne microtransmitters. Removing them would involve some massive hemorrhaging, so no."

"Damn. Well, we're gonna go."

"I've got notes. I'm giving you everything I've seen written and stolen about Cataclysm. You'll need it, and I'm hoping it will make some kind of sense to you."

"Judging from the way I've seen foreign words and things appear as familiar, there's a chance."

"Alright, enough stalling and waiting. I'm going to grab whatever I can from here and load up. Kaitlinn will be contacting Charista for a report and status, so that should give us enough time to make a break for it. We get Norg and Ashton and whoever else from the Action and make a run for it."

"I'll get a Landcrawler. It'll get us going, but I won't have time to disable the security algorithm. If they tap it, we'll be on foot."

"It's better than waiting on foot." I shrugged.

The Pull came back stronger. It stung like an electrical shock, but as soon as I stepped in that direction, every little bit I progressed that way, the better I felt. I just hoped that what I'd seen of Ana was in fact the future and not just some wishful daydream. She had to be alright, she just had to.

Kado closed up his P-LAD and put it in his bag. I took another drink of water before I gathered everything I could. The sight of Ana, alive and fighting, spurred me. The feeling I'd had of falling to earth was replaced with the sensation of my feet planted firm and me ready for another fight, like Ana would've been.

If we could just get to the Range and Cataclysm, it stood there, just urging me to get to it. My bargaining chip, their leverage. My ticket home.

"Kado, I'm not waiting anymore, I'm going for Cataclysm now."

"Yeah?"

I nodded. "Kaitlinn agreed to send me with a unit after I showed her how much I know about that area and where Cataclysm is, but she still wants to wait until her regiment is situated before we make a move. I can't shake the feeling I won't come back if she sends me with her people anyway. We need to get an upper hand here while there's one to get."

"Who's going with you?"

"So far, Norg. Would be great if we could get some help from you as well."

"Well, I'd feel better about getting these units moving, but if we can nab Cataclysm, so much the better."

I told Kado the rest of the plan, about the Valentium bait and going for Cataclysm.

"They want this Delivery, let's get it to them. They're glorified scavengers. They haven't been interested in killing us as much as they want their Valentium, so we're gonna deliver it to them," I said.

"Well, if that works, and we get Cataclysm in our hands, we'll really be sitting pretty. We won't be answering to anyone anymore." Kado grinned widely.

"Just better watch our end too," Kado said. "We've been through enough already, we need to be smart about this. There are enemies on all sides, even our own."

Chapter 9 (Ana)

THE FOOTSTEPS HEADED OUT of the room when the same voice burst over Eben's comm, this time doused in fear:

"Eben, get here now! Raiders!"

We looked at each other and wondered what that meant. Had Jacobs changed his mind and back tracked to us? Were we close to the Storehouse after all?

Our room guest's steps picked up downstairs and then there were loud pops from outside. After the noise, a roar built. Treg slid the door to the closet open and we crept back to the window for another look.

A large group of people appeared from the direction of the woods and moved toward the Omegans. Whoever they were, they weren't Jacobs' group. These soldiers looked ragged, with tattered clothing, most with faces twisted in anger. A few wore breathing masks. The roars and shouts came from them at random. A few carried pulse rifles, but most of 'em just had simple sticks or clubs.

"The hell kinda weapons are those?" Treg asked.

As we watched the makeshift weapons they carried, Dawn explained, "I told you, these groups are all over the Outlands. They do, take, and make whatever they need to survive, and that includes weapons."

Whatever rifles they had couldn't have been any better than the tech the Omegans tested. They descended on the Omegans like a pack of wild wolves, with no regard for the fact they were outgunned in every possible way.

The ones with pulse rifles aimed them at the Omegans, but they fired nothing. They must've been hit by that Darkness too. The Omegans laid down heavy fire on the ragged group, but that never fazed them. They chucked rocks and whatever they could at them, and charged right into the hail of pulse fire.

It was unreal.

One of the stones connected with the Disruptor, smashed it and sent it to the ground in several pieces. The barrage of Omegan fire hammered the ragged group and threw a few of 'em off balance. Some fell, but each one who could got back up charged more, even the wounded ones.

Were they even human?

One of them shouted, and the whole group took off in a sprint toward the Omegans, their voices raised in a collective war cry. Whoever they were, they had nothing that ID'ed them as Action or Coalition or even Lebabolis troops. I figured this was it; they'd be wasted in a quick heartbeat for that kinda behavior. But no, they kept up their fast pace, a loud chorus of yells and whoops. With no vehicles or heavy weapons on them, they ran blindly toward the Omegans.

If someone had described what I was looking at then, I'd have laughed in their face.

Yet there it was.

They ran forward, not walked, not headed for cover; they ran. The only thing they had going for them was more numbers. Even with their filthy appearance, their stance, the way they moved as if they were almost mechanical. Their motions looked like Radomet, but instead they were real flesh and blood.

How had we missed that big a group, just the three of us alone in the woods? And also, how had they missed us, and how would we be seen? Another enemy to be destroyed?

The ragged troops collided with the Omegans, and the brawl that erupted kicked up a cloud of dust like a low lying fog. Soon the scene was just a mixture of dirt, swung arms, shouts, loud smashes of stick, rock, fist and heads making contact. A few pulse shots from the Omegans rang out, but then came the cracking sound of pulse rifles snapped in two. The ragged troops broke rifles, theirs and the Omegans, with their bare hands.

Finally, a small group of Omegans, including the tall and short ones who'd checked on the Disruptor, peeled away from the melee and found their vehicle and hauled ass in reverse, but not before they fired a few shots back toward the wild ones.

The Omegans who weren't as fast got pummeled even more by the ragged soldiers, who laid them out on the ground. The rest of the Omegans piled into their vehicles and beat a hasty retreat.

"Who the hell are they?" I asked.

Dawn squinted toward the strange troops. "Nobody important. A random tribe of scavengers from the Outlands like we talked about."

Treg shook his head at the pile of mangled Omegan corpses. "Those aren't scavengers. I've fought scavengers. More to the point, I've chased away scavengers. They're human vermin, and they run at the first sight of trouble. This group didn't have a working pulse rifle, but they overran a unit that could've wasted them all. Not only that, they crushed a few—see those bodies, Dawn? Those skulls are crushed. That's brawn, muscle, sheer force. Those Omegan troops had explosives, enough to blast a square mile around us into vapor, but they were frightened. Whoever the wild ones are, they've been trained."

"I agree. That kinda crazy takes learning."

The ragged troops joined into a large crowd near the remains of the Disrupter and shouted; some of it was cheers, other parts a bit of a song. Then, in the middle of the crowd, a thin soldier swung a pole around in an arc with a tattered and faded flag attached to it. The flag was twisted at first, but it opened up as it waved.

It was the flag of the Valkyrie.

I pointed to the flag and eyed Dawn. "They're nobody, but

they just happen to have a Valkyrie flag?"

"I'm telling you both, they're scavengers. Treg, maybe you never happened upon some of the more violent ones before, but that's what we're looking at here. Yes, Ana, that's a Valkyrie flag. Don't you realize, scavengers steal whatever they can? Why do you think we protected Lebabolis all those years? To keep people like them out. They're barbarians."

"Or they're the ones Lebabolis expelled because they couldn't be controlled."

"You're not going to believe that's the Guard, are you?" Dawn laughed for a second, until she saw Treg and I hadn't joined in. Her smile faded. "Any scavenger or deviant could've found that flag out here. Think about it. How much did the Action steal from Lebabolis over the years?"

Dawn's eyes pleaded with me. I watched the celebration. "I'm interested in 'em. They annihilated a disruptor and made short work of a better armed unit with a few rocks, sticks, and their bare hands. At least we hate the same people." I shrugged.

"You realize they might not even know what Lebabolis or the Omegans are? How do you know they aren't here for what we are, food?"

"They were all over the fight. That was just brute force; maybe they were scavenging for food but they aren't right now."

"Fine, I'll suppose for a minute that they are the Guard. Look at them. They look crazy. What makes you so sure they won't attack us too? It would take no time for them to knock off three more people."

"She has a point, Ana. Besides, if they're really the Guard, Lebabolis threw them out. Why would they help us? To them, we're more of the same. They have no idea what the Action is, much less the Coalition. We'd look like Lebabolis military to them."

"I got you both. But they could just as well come up here and start rooting around like the Omegans were. We've made our play, and now we're here, dumb as it was. I say we face 'em. We're bound to come across the Omegans again. Wouldn't it be better having more numbers when we do?"

"You're reaching here, Ana. Letting them leave is prudent."

"Nah."

Dawn folded her arms. "So tell us how you expect to convince an angry mob you're a friendly."

"With this." I flung the knife up between Dawn and myself, then flipped it and caught the blade in my hand. I held the Valkyrie emblem to her face. "See, we got a matching set."

"You can't resist throwing yourself in it, can you?" Dawn asked.

"Honey, I've been in it. I want a way out. Hiding in some damned closet and cowering is what I did back in Lebabolis, and look where it's got me."

I blew past Dawn's extra warnings and curses and headed outside. My throat clenched up a bit. Sure, there wasn't any telling what they'd do once they saw me. They charged soldiers that out gunned them without any hesitation. What would they do to a single soldier? But something in me just said *go*.

The soldiers stood in a tight group and shouted when I approached. A few caught sight of me and their cheers melded into a distinctive growl. I held my arms up and walked up a few steps. I felt their eyes on me. Soon I was in the middle of them, a sea of vicious faces with smoky colored eyes that glared out at me like a sea of angry crystals.

The air was a nasty mix of body odor, blood, and from the look at their mouths, whatever these people ate for food. The pack of faces around me tightened in on me like wild animals ready for their next feast. I swallowed the tightness in my throat, took a breath, and heaved some words out over the roar of their bellows. "I come in peace—I'm against the soldiers you just smashed." They answered me with more grunts and groans like a pack of mad dogs.

Several of 'em glanced over my shoulder, and the voices picked up volume. I looked over to Treg and Dawn by the outside of the circle.

After a few minutes, a tall soldier made his way from around the others until he stood a foot from me. His gaze knifed into me. I swallowed hard but held steady.

The tall one eyed me up and down. His face was a collection of scars and cuts. His pulse rifle was slung across his back, not unlike how Treg carried his. He nudged a finger into the Coalition insignia on my chest plate. His voice was as ragged and gravel sounding as he looked. "What's that?"

"The Coalition."

"The what?"

"It's a truce between Lebabolis and the Action."

"The Action? Never heard of it. But we know about Lebabolis. You some kinda patrol?"

"No, Lebabolis is under Lock Down because of the Omegans." I gestured to the bodies on the ground.

"Oh them. Yeah, we come up on them sometimes and get the bastards running. They get off some shots and we take a few hits but not enough to stop us none." He let out a raspy laugh. "So Lebabolis... You're one of theirs, huh?" He laughed more and then swung his rifle down underneath my chin. "I hate Lebabolis. They threw us aside."

The cold steel of the barrel dug into the flesh of my neck. I felt the rattle of my pulse in my throat.

His nostrils flared. "We been scrapping for whatever and screwing up what we feel like just to make them regret the day they lost us. Fighting troops on the ground and shootin' their Hell Hawks outta the sky keeps us sharp, I 'spose. More so to be a knife in Charista's ass."

His eyes darkened as he pushed the barrel into my chin. The cool metal dug further into my flesh, and I felt my jaw press harder against the roof of my mouth. Around me, the growls increased. Through it I heard Treg's yells for them to back off, but it was useless. What the hell was I thinking?

Scarface's eyes widened in curiosity, and the barrel of the rifle pressed harder. Treg scuffled nearby and shouted, "We're fighting Omegans too; we want to destroy them!"

"Easy, boy," the tall soldier muttered. "How good a job you been doin' when they're still around?"

"We've got two Regiments of Lebabolis Warrior Products in maneuvers against them."

Scarface laughed more. "You're dreaming, all of you. You ain't stopping that lot."

"You did more just now than I'd seen in a good while." I gazed deep into his eyes.

Scarface returned my look with a stern glare. "We got lucky. Ain't always that way. Number and tech like Radomet won't stop them much either."

Treg said, "We're fighting them one at a time; it's all we can do."

"They're a disease. They'll keep going til we're wiped out. Only way of ending them is extermination. They'll never stop coming. They don't want anything but to wipe you out, don't you get that?" Scarface shook his head and looked around at his group. Some nodded in reply, the rest stood in place. A few shot me curious looks before they focused again on their leader. I hadn't won 'em over. Not yet, anyway.

"We won't stop 'em if we run. Besides, we got a deal with Lebabolis."

Scarface leaned in closer to me. My eyes watered under his rotten breath. "You mean you're their slaves. You served Lebabolis and you're still serving them as their army."

"Maybe, but it's how we stopped 'em from attacking us."

"It's the easy way."

"You got a better idea?" My eyes darted to the soldier with the flag. He held the pole up straight, the flag danced lazily in the slight breeze. "Why are you waving the Valkyrie flag?"

"What do you care?" Scarface held his rifle firmly. Beads of sweat tickled and itched my forehead as they snaked downward toward my neck.

"Because of this."

I twisted my hand back and grabbed the dagger and slowly unsheathed it. At the sound of the blade's ring of being set free, the tall soldier activated his rifle again. "One more move and I'm gonna fry the inside of your skull."

I gripped the knife and managed a small grin. One of the other ragged soldiers to my right gasped. "Where'd she get that?" Another one said. The murmurs spread until the tall soldier glanced down and saw the knife. His eyes widened, and he pulled his rifle back.

"Baudricort of the Action gave it to me for protection."

Scarface shouldered his rifle. They watched the knife like a sacred relic. He held a hand up and quieted his troops then turned back to me. "That knife belonged to the Valkyrie. Our leader. My name's Duncan. I'm commander of this—"

"The Guard?"

Duncan shrugged. "What's left of it. Banished by Lebabolis because we refused to follow anyone but the Valkyrie, the true Valkyrie. We been in the Outlands for over twenty years now, living off the land and taking what we needed to survive. Lebabolis wouldn't have us, but they knew better than to toy with us."

"You were their army, correct?"

"We served with the Valkyrie, and the Valkyrie served Lebabolis. We were the protectors of Lebabolis, and we gave the Omegans plenty to think about. There was no stopping us. We faced them down with the Valkyrie and turned their forces back."

"Well, you and Cataclysm," I said.

"We beat them down enough. You think you're tough, sneaking in and around here, gettin' into a scrap now and then, getting some shots off? You aren't hard. You gotta eat, breathe, and sleep soldierin'. Omegans don't take any rest. They stab you, you shoot them. They shoot you, you blast them and send them straight into hell. Period. Cataclysm finished what we started, but you best listen, foolin' with that is meddling with powers that shouldn't be tested."

"Yeah, well, how did you lose Cataclysm?"

Duncan thrust a finger toward me as if it was a blade. "We didn't lose it! The Valkyrie knew it meant trouble. That kind of power shouldn't be in anyone's hands. Besides, we had things in hand and we sent them Omegans to hell right good."

"As you saw, not forever," I said. "They're back for Valentium and payback."

"So I see, but it ain't our concern. I won't fight for a country that abandoned us; neither will they."

I looked at their group and realized how much we were alike, two groups of people who were cast out by the same country. "What about the Action then? We aren't Lebabolis. We're like you, sick of lives we're forced into. We broke free from Lebabolis and we've been struggling. The Action wants freedom too, from a system that treats people like parts. We're trying to get to the Western Range and stop the Omegans."

Duncan's eyes softened, and I saw even a trace of humanity under them. He looked on me with warmth. "What's your name, fiery girl?"

"Ana Crucinal."

"You got spirit, Ana Crucinal. But this fight is yours, not ours. We done our bit for country, and paid a price we didn't deserve. Now we just want to survive in peace."

"You weren't peaceful a few seconds ago. Hell, you almost did me in." I scoffed.

"We show force and take what we need, but no more. We're not marauders, rapists or ravagers. We scavenge to survive. We hunt and use our will to survive to determine our course. Nothing more."

"I told you." Dawn shrugged.

Duncan's friendly gaze went furious in an instant as he looked toward Dawn. "You shut your mouth, gray band. You're a pawn and you know it. I got a good mind to shove this here stick down your throat, see how it tastes to ya."

I waved my hands. "If you think you'll survive with the Omegans around, you're kidding yourself. You said the words, they're brutal and they won't stop. They want Valentium, and revenge, but I've seen them up close. How can you walk from a fight like this? If the Omegans win, they'll bleed this land dry, and anyone they come across is dead meat. "

"And Lebabolis won't do the same?" Duncan asked.

I swallowed hard on that truth. "We'll figure that out when the time comes. I know we can take control if you help us. You were the elite once. You stood up to Omegans even though they were tougher, and you held them off. You became what was needed when it mattered. I'm just asking you to do it again.

"For what?" Duncan asked.

I thrust the knife into the air. "A chance to say you didn't lie down when it was most important. One last chance to make the Guard name mean something again. Omegans won't be satisfied when Lebabolis and the Action are no more; they'll keep going until the world is under their rule. Think your peaceful existence of just taking what you need will keep you out of their way? They'll come for you. Not now, not this month, but there will come a time. They'll be on you and it'll be too late. I've been on the run most of my life. I wanted for a long time more than anything to just leave this behind. But they took my brother and other sick people. They made me fight. I hate 'em for it, but I hate the Omegans even more. And there'll be a time to pay back Lebabolis too, I guarantee you."

I felt their eyes on me and thought I'd made a breakthrough with 'em, but Duncan set things straight again. "Lebabolis can crumble into the sea for all we care."

"They aren't going anywhere soon, especially once they get Cataclysm," I said.

"What do you mean, get Cataclysm?" Duncan's brow creased.

"That's what I said."

Duncan asked, "They found it?"

"Baudricort showed me, showed us."

"Impossible. It was hidden long ago, before you were born, and we've had no idea where."

"It's not only possible, but we know where it is, and we're gonna deliver it to 'em." I grimaced at the idea but reminded myself it wasn't the final plan.

I heard a ripple of chuckles through the nearby Guard soldiers. Duncan shook his head. "Are you mad?"

"No, I'm trading for something else."

"What, exactly?" Duncan's held his hands in the air.

"I don't know."

"You don't know? What the hell are you thinking then; you just want to start trouble? You might be better off with us instead of followin' some fool leader gonna toss you away soon as you give them what they need. You're high on hope, fiery girl."

"I'm against a wall; hope's all I got."

Duncan paced back and forth. He scratched his head and looked at me for a few moments in silence. "The Omegans aren't to be taken light. They're pretty fierce, and we seen that weapon of theirs. It's ruined more than a few of what we got left of our people, so I know exactly what you're saying, believe me."

Aggravation settled in on me, and I fought with myself to keep in this talk. If I flew off and left here, I'd have lost the one ally I needed most. I braced myself and focused my mind on what Baudricort would've said to them. "We get Cataclysm; even if we have to give it to 'em, we're in control."

"No, you're giving up control. You don't understand, that kind of power don't belong in one person's hands, no matter who they are."

"If we don't get this, and someone else like her does, there's no telling what'll happen. Someone's gotta try," I said.

"And you're crazy enough to. So you got a plan, and you're crazy enough to think it'll work?"

"It might, if we get some help."

"From who, us?"

I scanned the group again. "Yeah. Look, I've seen and read a lot about you. The Guard were the toughest fighters Lebabolis has ever known. When I was a kid I heard the stories, how it took three Radomet to stop a Guard member any day of the week. Yeah, times have changed, you're older and slower, but think about what you did. And what did you do to get there? It wasn't just your training, or your physical strength, even your belief in the Valkyrie. It was your hearts. They're pure and full of devotion. You don't just fight to kill. You fight to survive, to protect. Because you care, you've got loved ones. And you'd die before you let anyone get over on you. Fighting for something is more powerful than fighting against it. You became the fiercest warriors through training and service and belief in the Valkyrie. You can do it again, if you want to. And

I think you do. I don't think this life you've got, scavenging around for scraps, taking pot shots at crafts that aren't even aware or can fight back to any degree is what you want. You want more. And that's what we want. We're finishing what was started by the Valkyrie. And we could really use the help. How about it?"

Duncan gazed at me for a long time. His troops had eyes fixed on me too. Their scowls melted into more thoughtful expressions. "Sorry, fiery girl. The Valkyrie is dead."

I thought about the voice and what it told me, but would they have even believed it? Maybe it was just a ghost from years back and I was lucky enough to be the haunted one. If I told people, they would've just dismissed me as this crazy girl with big plans and, as a bonus, who, oh yeah, heard voices. Who the hell would follow someone like that?

I shrugged that off though and kept on. "It's up to you. I can't make you. But you faced down an enemy that could've easily laid waste to you with no fear. We need your force."

Duncan sighed, and his head dipped a little. "We're scattered halfway across the Outlands. Even the Guard isn't one group anymore. We do what we need to survive."

"You won't survive much longer like this. Somebody's gonna fire Cataclysm. If not me, then her, and you remember what Cataclysm does, right?" I said.

"Yeah." Duncan sighed.

"Charista's turning it on the Omegans first chance she gets, and you and I know she won't stop there. She wants the whole world to fall under this umbrella of Lebabolis."

Duncan folded his arms. "Worlds fall all the time, fiery girl. We fought our fight. It's someone else's turn now." He laughed. "We're headed home; our round of foraging is done for now. I don't expect you'll see us again."

My eyes pled with them, but it was useless. Duncan gave a shrill whistle and his troops joined up together. As one, they swiveled back in the direction of the woods and marched off. A loud chorus of "One or None" followed them, and a wave of sadness hit me. Was it that hard, convincing them? Had I just failed again? Who would've thought I was any kinda leader if they'd seen me here right now? Was the Action really that much different than the Guard? Was I looking at our future, my future… a member of a bunch of scavengers who prowled the world like a starving pack of dogs just in for whatever the next scrap of meat to be stolen? How could they have used the same cry, the same call that was ingrained in the Action? Would I be a ragged, worn out leader of a troop of renegades just scraping by for whatever we could get to sustain ourselves?

"Satisfied?" Dawn asked.

"Better we ask than never know," I replied. "I thought they could've been up to the task."

"Wrong again. Let's go."

I nodded, my eyes still on the soldiers. I hated that they wouldn't or couldn't stay, and I wondered about what I'd seen behind Duncan's eyes. They said a lot more than his words, but that was just a mystery, maybe forever unsolved. His gaze was clouded with something else, like smokiness inside an otherwise clear crystal.

Chapter 10 (Nelson)

"NELSON, WHILE WE STILL have time, there's one more thing I need to show you." Kado ushered me over to his terminal and pulled up the MODOSNet screen. He studied me with the sincere gaze of a therapist. "First, tell me again what Baudricort told you about Ana."

I thought back to those last moments with him on the floor in his busted out quarters. The smoke that wafted around from the blast itched my nose and the ringing in my ears from being so close to the explosion made it tough to make anything out. He was a mixture of emotions: fear of dying without knowing if what he had done made any difference. He was all worry and uncertainty. But I leaned in close enough for his last few words about Ana. "He just said to watch out for her."

Kado eyed me, expressionless. "Ana's a mystery to a lot of people. I know Treg trained her. But her skill, her strength, that's ingrained in Warrior Products from birth, and before. That's the whole idea of the Product system: traits survive, even if free choice doesn't. Me, I never bought she was a Worker Product. She was too strong. It takes more than training to get as capable as she is."

I nodded. "Treg once told me she took on a Radomet by herself."

"That's what I mean. Once the Action started, Baudricort corrupted records to keep as many people safe so they never knew the system had been compromised for people like Ana."

He then went back to his terminal. "I'm not sure why this was hidden, but our friend Ana's got a lot more going on than any of us could've guessed."

"What do you mean?"

"Baudricort never said anything to me about what I'm about to show you."

He leaned back from the screen, and I had a look. There was the MODOSNet file on Ana on the screen. Her parent entries were blank. "This happened for a lot of the Action members; Baudricort saw to it when he was wreaking havoc in the system during Exodus."

"So what, Kado? I don't understand; she's got these skills, but is she really any different from the rest who escaped? Baudricort just gave her a head start, like the others."

"Ahh, maybe. And sure, that's a safe guess. See, Lebabolis would do whatever they could to hunt down people, even if it meant tracking down their parents. But I didn't show you this so you could see what was removed." He tapped a few more controls. "I want you to see what was never in that record."

With that, he activated a video, and I found myself staring once again into the eyes of Baudricort.

"Ana, my daughter. I'm a coward. I held things from you. I thought I was protecting you, but I was really protecting myself. But now, I want to be clear. If what I think has happened, you need to be ready because you've got work to do.

"I wish I had time to tell you everything you've wanted to know about your life and where you came from. But there was never enough time. I'm marked, and I don't know how much time I have left. Your mother—"his voice wavered and he suppressed a sob—"is probably dead by now, so I must pass this onto you. I couldn't risk telling you sooner, and give Charista the chance to do a Link pull on you. But you must know her name is—"

The video crackled and the image popped blank for several

seconds.

"You've gotta be kidding me." Kado adjusted and tweaked controls, but it was useless.

"I don't know what happened. Was he making this right before he died? Maybe it was a Valentium spike."

"Can't say for sure. Wait—here it comes again."

The video resumed but nothing further about Ana's mother.

"I've made so many mistakes. But maybe, if you're still alive and seeing this, there's still a chance we'll stop the bigger catastrophe. My only hope is Charista hasn't found out who you are yet. I'm even taking a risk saying this to you now, but it's time you know. I'm sorry it's too late for me to tell you in person. Cataclysm is the deadliest weapon and I was ordered... forced to create it by Charista. I used data she'd gotten from the Omegans, it... was always supposed to be secret, but I don't see the point of keeping that hidden anymore.

"Charista's the one you need to watch out for. She'll say whatever she needs; don't believe her. She'll tell you she's the Valkyrie. Watch yourself; she's also gotten into the Action with her spies somewhere, I'm sure of it. It feels like there's someone in this group who's not one of us. I just hope I figure out who before it's too late.

"I've left information with Kado on the Cataclysm device and a security system I've enacted with the Valkyrie. Cataclysm will not fire without the Failsafe enacted. I don't want to say exactly how it works here in case this is being monitored. You must get to Cataclysm and use the Failsafe system before anyone else can, or the destruction that happened before will happen again on a much bigger scale. And if Charista is in control of it, there'll be no end. She'll destroy whoever's against her: the Action, the Omegans, anyone else who doesn't fit her plan. It's vital you follow the details in the fail-safe method I've outlined."

The tears rolled free down his face and his voice got strained into a plaintive whine. "I wish I could've given you the life you wanted or deserved. You needed love from your birth parents, but you had none. You needed a family, but it was taken from you. You needed security, but you only had hiding and deception. I wish it could've been different, that I could adjust things, make things better, I do. But even with the Verges, some things still can't be done over."

"Just know, Ana—it's in your blood. You're stronger than I, your mother or anyone else. The fate of Cataclysm rests with you. It's in your blood to survive, to manage, to do whatever needs to be done to outlast the rest.

"Your mother was in danger as I was. We were two different products and weren't allowed to breed. But we loved each other. We wanted no part of a system that made such demands on people. But we knew also that we weren't able to get away just then. So we did the next best thing. We hid, we gathered resources, we bided our time. One by one, the Action grew until we were strong enough to leave. But Lebabolis wasn't oblivious. It didn't take long before their spies and scouts infiltrated us, and your mother was one of the casualties.

"I'm so sorry for everything. I only wanted to get you out, and when we did I thought just maybe I hadn't failed you both. I hoped you'd one day do what we never could and turn the evil of Lebabolis on them. You are my heart, soul and my message to Charista. I know you'll make things right.

"You'll have to fight harder and survive more and go further than we've been able to. But in the end, I know you'll be the one standing over the rest. Just remember, no matter what happens, you'll always be my daughter and I love you with all I am."

The screen flickered and faded to black. A lump formed in my throat as the words hung in the air. "I love you with all I am."

I stared at the blank screen and wondered what Ana knew about this. I felt memories of Mom push through with Baudricort's message. I wanted to hug Ana right then. How much must it have hurt her all those years, never knowing, that missing piece of her like a window missing a pane of glass? I realized how lucky I'd been, at least to have known my mom while she was alive.

"She never mentioned her mother at all," I said.

"When we left, our lives were uprooted, connections severed. Some families were even split among loyalties to Lebabolis and the Action. Even though we've rejoined, breaches like that aren't repaired as easily."

"We've got to get to her. If she's alive, she's headed to the Lebabolis capital and if she's there now, who knows what Charista is telling her?"

"It's not quite that simple." He smiled in a pained wince and drooped brow. He activated some more screens, and several items flashed up on the screen. Words in a faded green stared back at me, and Kado maneuvered his hands for awhile until there on screen was a message between Charista and the Omegans.

"Those coordinates are familiar," I muttered, my eyes agape.

"Yeah? How so?"

"That's where Llewyn and the Action are heading. Why is Charista sharing this information with the Omegans?"

"And look, there she's mentioning something about delivery of a package. What is she talking about?"

"It couldn't be Cataclysm, could it?"

"No, there's no way. She wants that all to herself."

"Maybe it's the Coalition. She's been sending us up all this time. She doesn't want a truce or even to let the Action exist outside; she's not stupid. She'll just set us up to be her enemy again someday. No, this package is us; she's delivering the Coalition to the hands of the Omegans."

"But for what? Would they go for that? They just want to destroy us anyway."

"There must be some reward in it for them as well. No one does something of that magnitude without the idea of getting something in return."

"So we're collateral? She's going to get Cataclysm and use it on the Omegans and us now?"

"Maybe she found a way to invert the mechanism."

Norg and Ashton returned. A trail of bluish smoke snaked from the end of the weapon.

"Well?" Kado asked.

Norg looked at the weapon for a second, then back to us with a mixture of a glare and a grin. "Uniquely badass. Ya done good."

"That's a relief! Nelson and I've been doing our own bit of research here."

"Yeah, how so?" Ashton asked.

"According to what Nelson's telling me, Cataclysm is in a grouping away from the Range, so we've got a shot of getting it if we can sneak over there undetected."

Norg said, "Well, what are we waiting for? You tell him Kaitlinn's on her way?"

I nodded. "Yeah, so I'm thinking we take a small group, me, Norg, Kado, a few others, and load Cataclysm onto a Hell Hawk and make our way to a safe point."

Kado's head hung. His body shook with exhaustion.

"How many hours she's had you working at all this?" I asked.

His eyes were a mix of watery and twitchy. He didn't answer me; his eyes did enough talking anyway.

"Too much for too long. I wish I had more answers or knew what to suggest to you. I-I'm sorry."

"No, no." I went to his side. "None of this is your fault. We're all being used here; that's why it's more important than ever we try this."

"There's a lot of open ground between here and there." Kado sighed. "What if we get attacked? Even with these new weapons, the Omegans won't need a lot to overpower us."

"It's risky, but what have we done that isn't?"

Norg patted Kado's arm. "He's right, man. We gotta book it on this one. Longer we stay around jabberin' and debating plans, the sooner they could happen on it. Don't think they don't have their own kinda scans running neither."

When Norg mentioned scams, Kado's face brightened a bit. "There's something else you need to know. Word from Kaitlinn is they're setting up a decoy for the Omegans. A lure. They're hoping they'll bite for the Valentium; we're putting a lot out. They'll move their deposits of Valentium to a location a good thirty miles from the Cataclysm point."

Norg shook his head. "What else aren't they telling us? I'm sick of waiting; let's go!"

Kado glanced off a bit. "Are they even sure the Omegans will go for this Valentium decoy?"

I shrugged. "Valentium hauls have been their MO of late. You weren't there for the crater attack. They had us boxed in and they let us out of there. We're giving them a nice bit of Valentium just served right up to them. It's gonna work."

Kado looked at the weapon, then back to me. His brow crinkled and he took a slow breath. "It's a risk no matter what we do. But if we nab Cataclysm, I'll figure out that Failsafe and get it to work."

Norg grinned. "If anybody can, it's you, brain child."

"Let me see that." I reached for the notes from Kado. The words on the page were gibberish alright. They were in some other language. But I just stared at the page like I did for the map, and it happened.

The letters flickered and then they rearranged themselves to me as English. I read notes from Baudricort that he had entered about the Failsafe. It was set up and tied to the Valkyrie. They prevented the operation of the Cataclysm device unless the Failsafe was triggered by transmitters located in her blood.

I said, "Kado, it's tied to her blood, the Valkyrie. The weapon's useless without it."

"What?" Kado grabbed the notes and eyed them. "We don't even know the Valkyrie is still alive. She'll work on a hack of course. We don't even know if she's aware of this Failsafe."

Norg grunted. "So let's move out then. I'm tired of waiting around for something to happen to us."

The screen rifled through a lot of different displays. Pictures, faces, details rushed past me like water over a waterfall. Then, when I got dizzy, the display jerked to a halt and there were two faces: Ana and another woman I'd never seen before.

"Baudricort was keeping the Action safe," Kado explained. "Part of that was hiding the true identities of as many people in the Action as he could, even if it meant wiping their records. This was especially for anyone Lebabolis would consider important."

Kado jabbed a finger toward the strange woman's picture. "This is Petra. I know she doesn't mean anything to you"—he glanced at me—"but she means a lot to us. She led the group that turned back the Omegans all those years ago."

I sat up. "The Valkyrie?"

Kado nodded. "And no one really knows whatever happened to her. Some say she was murdered, others say she was delivered to the Omegans as a bribe."

I said, "If I can't be with her, I figure I'm as safe as I'd be, being with you guys. You're part of the Circle, and that's good enough for me."

"So let's do this." Norg motioned to the door.

I grabbed Kado's arm. "We need to move on this now. The Omegans don't have to wait for anything. They are pressing on, and the more we wait the more time they have to get a foothold. We'll try and reach Llewyn and fill him in; he'll be at the Range soon and we need to get moving now!"

"Get moving where?" Her gruff voice entered the room before she did. The door swung open and there was Kaitlinn. Kado swallowed hard and managed a nod in her direction. The air in the room seemed to freeze. Kaitlinn tossed me a dirty look as she meandered toward us. "Some day you'll learn your safety is one of my biggest concerns." She glanced toward the weapons and then to Kado. "I trust you've tested them out thoroughly?"

"Yes, ma'am. Been through all I could put them through, given the short time frame."

"We need these passed out to the rest of the crews. I'm sending a few people out on this. For now I want you back on the facilities issue, alright? We need to get them running so we can keep our group moving."

"Affirmative." Kado nodded.

Kaitlinn looked at me. "You're coming with me, Nelson. We're going to check with Llewyn on his location. He's run into problems, and we need further assistance with the terrain and your knowledge of that area before we start for Cataclysm."

Chapter 11 (Ana)

"ENOUGH DISTRACTIONS." Dawn shoved branches out of her way and walked deeper into the woods. "We could've been killed back there. You've no idea how unpredictable those people are."

"Those people?"

"The Guard, alright?"

"So you do know them."

"Yes, Ana, I do. You keeping score? Any more foolish detours you've got to suggest?"

"We needed food. Seemed a reasonable risk."

Dawn's annoyed gaze pierced into me and made me wonder just what kind of plans she had for us at the Capital. Her eyes flickered for a second, and I wondered, once I mentioned the Guard, why she brushed it off so fast.

"You knew they were still out here, didn't you? Your talk about random bands was you trying to scare us off looking for anyone. All this time, you knew. Did you contact 'em, get 'em to join you? Oh, I bet that went well. You send a messenger and what, they broke their arms?"

Her eyes darted about, then they gazed back in the direction we came. She looked back at her P-LAD, but I yanked her hand, and we were face to face again. "Well?"

"We always suspected. The Action was our bigger concern.

We gave the Guard up for lost. Our recon groups, when they came across any of them, it looked like what you saw back there. Can you blame us, I mean, you did see how they were right? That's how they've been. They sustained themselves and kept out of our way for the most part. Charista figured they'd eventually waste away."

"Unlike the Action? Why'd you even bother with the Action when you had them?"

"We didn't need another group of Renegades, and you were still close enough to the fold. You weren't wiped out."

"Neither are they. They're hanging tough, even away from Lebabolis this long."

"Seems so. But trust me, you don't want to be involved with them. There's no guarantee when the fight comes down to it that they'll step up, and they just might turn on you."

"How do you know?"

"Because we tried it with the Guard. We went to them years ago when they scrounged like rats and made the offer: give us another go, all will be forgotten. We offered them a chance to utilize their potential. The Omegans hadn't returned by then, but security was always a priority for Charista. The Guard took off shortly after. Living like they do, it changes you. They aren't what they were; I hope for once you'll believe me here."

Her gruff dismissal of this group surprised me. Everything I had heard about the Guard was they were extremely fierce and had been the thing that stood between Lebabolis and the Omegans for all those years. I wondered what about the Action other than our general age made us a better choice. What happened to this group that turned them into what I'd seen? Is that what we would become if things didn't end well for us in this war?

Dawn darted back out ahead as our walk continued. I fell back near Treg. "Some afternoon, huh?"

"Yeah, for sure. You good?" His brow wrinkled, a concerned look on his face.

"Pretty much. Never came up against the Guard before."

"Me either. You did great, seeing as you had a rifle at your throat."

"He wasn't gonna use it. He was testing me."

"You think?"

"Yeah, I do."

"Come on. You saw what they did to the Omegans. I can still hear the sound of one of those arms popping. He'd have mangled you if you hadn't shown that knife."

"Treg, no way."

"Why are you so sure?"

"They've been used to scavenging and they respond when there's danger, like an animal would. They survive and fight only when they have to. Yeah, they sized me up. But once they saw who we were, and that we weren't scared, and I had the knife—"

"Which could've been taken off a dead body. Hell, that's what they've been doing for years."

"The Guard was the absolute in everything. Strength, loyalty, bravery. He tested me. It was in his eyes."

"Or, you just lucked up."

"Wish they would've taken me up on joining us."

"You're thinking about who they were. You gotta see what they have become, a bunch of wasted out renegades. They've been away in the woods too long. I don't think Duncan's all there in the head, if he ever was."

"No food, Treg."

"Huh?"

"The food. The rations, what we went there for. They never took anything off us. That didn't seem odd to you?"

"They could've found theirs somewhere else. Speaking of, let's grub while we walk."

I slid a ration bar over my lips. The sweet and salty flavor melted on my tongue. The flavor mixed with my saliva as it drizzled down my throat until my stomach warmed at the first food it had had in days. I took a few quick bites until I gagged and slowed down to a moderate nibble. In mere minutes I felt eons better. We munched as we walked. Dawn went behind us and followed in silence. After a mile into the woods, I waited until she neared me. She looked at me and eyed the ration bar I offered her.

"Come on, it's why we stopped."

Her glance darted between me and the food for a second. Soon, her mouth quivered, and a bit of saliva formed on her lips. Her tongue slipped from between her lips as if she were a snake ready for its next meal. She then grasped the protein and hungrily devoured it.

I couldn't hide the smirk on my face and didn't want to either. "Looks like Treg and I weren't the only ones starving."

She spoke between bites. "Can't risk that again." She chewed a bit more and flashed a quick eye to me. "Thank you."

I pulled her chin until her eyes returned to mine. "I'm believing your story about being stuck with us against your will. I still don't like you on that thing so much, like it's a beacon to Charista you're not telling us about. But I also figure the sooner we get there, the sooner you and I don't have to see each other again."

We made it back to the deep woods just as night fell. The moonlight was scattered among the branches and leaves above us. We made our way slowly through small pockets of dim light. The breeze had picked up by then, and I had my hands thrust under my shoulders.

I motioned to Dawn. "Let's stop for now and rest. I'd rather not stumble across an Omegan patrol in the dark. We'll regroup in the morning."

"Alright. I have to admit that's not a bad idea," Dawn replied.

I smirked. "Well, small favors."

Treg cleared the branches and leaves, and made a space between the trees with smooth ground so the three of us had a spot for the night.

"We still going the right way?" I asked Dawn.

The light from Dawn's P-LAD cast the only light around us besides the moon.

"Hmm, yeah, looks that way. We should hit it in another day."

The bushes made a soothing rustle in the wind. I was just

about to lean back and get comfortable when I heard a quick shuffle of branches off to the right from us, about ten feet away. It wasn't light enough to see much, and I saw nothing, not even any dim shapes. I jumped up, but the noise stopped and was replaced by the whisper of the wind again.

Dawn tapped her P-LAD and mouthed, "Ambush." My chest tightened, and I did my best to stop the tremor that had started.

I crawled over to Treg.

"What's goin on, Dawn acting stupid?" he asked.

"We heard something."

He looked around the area. "She scan for heat sigs?"

I nodded toward Dawn and twisted my hand in a circle with one finger pointed up. She held her P-LAD up and turned in the direction I showed her. Graphical images of the woods around us cascaded by on the screen. But then, a glowing dot of red and yellow made her stop in place. We looked at each other.

"Looks like one. Might be a vehicle if they're close enough."

"Great, and no guns." My hand slipped to the handle. "What you thinking, Treg?"

He looked around again, his eyes wide, but the thick blackness and dim light from the moon covered everything in a dull dark shroud. "If they're this close, they're watching us too, and we'd have heard from them by now. I think it's a lost patrol."

"Or the Guard snooping around," Dawn said.

"They wouldn't waste time here. It's too easy pickings at the housing units right now." The woods were covered in a blanket of darkness. The branches offered a slight rustle with the little breezes of wind that slipped around us.

The sound happened again, much closer this time. My face flushed from the heat, and I drew my blade. There wasn't time to run anywhere. Whoever or whatever it was moved in quickly. I stood up over Dawn. Treg clutched the muzzle end of his pulse rifle and held it out like a club. I planted my feet and held the knife in a fighting stance.

The rustling stopped once again.

"Who is it?" I whispered into the night air.

Nothing came in response for a few minutes. Then another

voice whispered, just above the sound of the breeze, "One..."

I looked at Treg. He replied, "Or none."

The branches rustled again, and the dull outline of a figure stepped out. It was a woman, and I caught sight of her face when a sliver of moonlight passed over her. She had high cheekbones, slender eyes that were fixed and alert like a hungry tigress, and a smirk I would know from anywhere.

Nycole.

"So you survived the crash too." I sheathed my blade. "Where the hell you been?"

"I was thrown free before the landing. Had to get my bearings."

"You could've made contact with us a little sooner."

"Well, how about you? You weren't waving a Valkyrie banner around or anything."

She scoffed and sat. "Anybody got a gun? I'm feeling naked without one."

"Nope, all we got are two dead sticks."

"Well, that sucks."

"Even more when you hear how."

Dawn nodded. "Hello there."

Nycole's brow raised a bit, but she returned the greeting. "Hey yourself."

We figured it was getting too late, and after the food we'd gotten we needed rest. Even Dawn agreed with that one. We made a camp out of a few close tree trunks and some fallen branches. Nycole gave us the scoop on her story. She'd bailed out before we hit ground—she was up top with Jacobs on the nav when she punched out. She came across what sounded like the same Omegan patrol we did. She hadn't made contact but fired a few long range shots their way before her gun got zapped when they activated Darkness.

"He wanted to land that bird. The personnel hold was more secure from a crash but not so much the cockpit. Crazy bastard. Refused the help I offered."

"They have a disruptor," I said with a mouthful of food. "We saw 'em test it. Took our weapons out."

Her eyebrows raised. "Not good. But your P-LAD wasn't affected?"

"No." Dawn flipped the device around. "Guess it was set for weapons only."

Nycole sat with us in a circle, her legs folded beneath her. She held a twig and traced random shapes on the ground with it. "We called them Darkness in the Warrior Product weapons program. Lebabolis was working on that while I was still over there, but they hadn't perfected it. Either the Omegans did it or they stole it. We had some intel on them they'd been working on how to fine tune it, to take out weapons and leave other tech functional."

I said, "Looks like they perfected it."

"So what are you doing out here by yourselves? Jacobs and the rest made it?" Nycole asked.

"Yeah, Jacobs and a good twenty others. He grabbed them and went off to find a Storehouse so they could get back to the fight," Treg said.

"He mutinied? Thought we were set to go for Cataclysm once we got clear of the Omegans," Nycole said.

Dawn sighed. "He had other ideas."

"Crazy jackass. Wouldn't be surprised if he were in custody now." Nycole chuckled.

Dawn snickered. "That's what I tried to tell them."

Nycole asked, "So what's the plan now; you three going for Cataclysm?"

"The plans changed a bit. We lost Nelson too. He was supposed to be with us, but we got separated back in the Crater," Dawn said.

"We're going for the Capital," I said.

Treg eyed me but said nothing. He returned to his meal.

Nycole looked at us. "The Capital is in Lock down. You think they'll just crack the door if you ask nice? They're probably under siege!"

I said, "We're a long way from Cataclysm, on foot with no weapons. What other choice we got?"

"I can come up with a few." Nycole shrugged.

127

I said, "You don't get it. I made an agreement with Charista."

Nycole said, "No, you don't get it, Worker Product, so let me enlighten you. You don't get into the Capital on a Lockdown. Damn, I've got more access than Ms. Laboratory over there, and I'm not sure I could even do it."

I grabbed a handful of leaves and tossed them to my side. "We have to try."

Nycole eyed the three of us. "Well, good for you. You have any idea how risky that is? You realize they're expecting people trying that? At a minimum the Omegans would be doing whatever to bust in, and you think you'll just be waltzing right in like nothing's wrong and you just want to say hello?"

I said, "I never said it'd be easy. But it's necessary."

"Why the Capital anyway?" Nycole asked.

"It's our deal," Dawn said.

Nycole swiped a hand toward Dawn. "Screw the deal. Charista doesn't have any ships; this Intellectual's just tired of running. What's Kaitlinn or Jacobs gonna say? It's their job to clear a path for you to Cataclysm."

"Jacobs knows; he even tried talking me out of it. And besides, neither of them's here now, are they?" I flung my hands up. "We made a deal for getting Cataclysm, and things got blown to hell. Besides, why are you so interested in not going back?"

Nycole shook her head. "It's the wrong direction, in more ways than one."

I said, "Yeah, or maybe you don't want to go back because it's not in your plans or worse, we aren't expected back there since we were supposed to die when you blew our Hell Hawk up. Is that it, Nycole? Real handy how you bailed out before we landed. Did Jacobs even know about the bomb? I bet he didn't."

Nycole cut her eyes at me. "You're ridiculous. Jacobs wouldn't have let the ship land if he was in on it. Don't be crazy."

I said, "Dawn says Charista's got transport ships at the Capital, so we're headed there. Besides, where can we find better weapons? I'd rather avoid the Easter egg hunt, me."

Nycole sipped her water and wiped her mouth on her sleeve. "Yeah, but getting through security won't be easy. Not even for mister silent entry over here."

Treg snorted a bit. "Told her it was pretty damned impossible, but she ain't changin' her mind."

I debated how much I should tell her or any of them about the voice. I never knew for sure if it was just something through the Link or not, anyway. And she wasn't one to leave with the Action, even when Treg did. I held off.

But Nycole, I just was never sure where I stood with her.

We continued the next morning on our twisting journey through the forest. The roads were nearby, and we used them as a guide but kept off them since the Omegans were always around. I wondered what that test was all about and if anyone knew about it. Charista and Kaitlinn always had good intel on the Omegans, but they never mentioned that little detail. I'd think a weapon that could've shut down every piece of tech we had, even MODOSNet, would've been worth a mention.

Chapter 12 (Nelson)

"I DON'T THINK SO." Norg aimed his pulse rifle right at Kaitlinn's chest. Her guards stood by, their rifles fixed on Norg. Kaitlinn's eyes widened, a frown etched into her face. "Just what do you think you're doing?"

Norg smirked. "We're going for Cataclysm; we ain't into your timetable anymore."

"Do you have short term memory loss? How do you expect to make it that far with just the two of you?"

"Make that three," Kado said.

"Oh, now I know you're forgetting things. Kado, we discussed your Link. I'm fully capable of blowing up a blood vessel in your brain, remember?"

"No, I remember pretty well, Kaitlinn."

"Don't try me. You've done a lot of good here and kept the Coalition running, but so help me if you do this, it's going to be the end of you. You'll be dead before you leave the compound."

"We're leaving and you can't stop us."

"You're committing suicide is what you're doing. You go out there and the Omegans find you, you'll be a blob of bloody matter when they're done."

"That's a chance I'm willing to take," I said. "I still don't see why you're so scared to go for it right now."

"It's too risky, Nelson. You have to understand all the moving parts here. You're not responsible for all these soldiers like I am."

The soldiers stepped toward Norg with their guns raised. Kaitlinn activated something on her vest and an alarm buzzed. More soldiers filled the room. "Subdue them! Leave Forrester and Kado alive, and kill Norg!"

Kado grasped one of his guns, flicked the controls on it, and fired it at Kaitlinn. A loud crackling hum filled the room, and a ball of glowing blue light leapt out the muzzle and surrounded Kaitlinn and the troops. They twitched for a few seconds then all of them let out a collection of shrieks and yells before they dropped to the floor. A few more seconds and the ball disappeared.

"What the hell was that?" Norg looked at Kado with wild eyes.

"Stun pulse; they'll be out for a few minutes. We gotta move fast. Grab what you can and let's go!"

We filed out of the building and trucked it over to the nearest Hell Hawk. Norg blasted the soldiers nearby, and we jumped aboard.

A familiar voice sounded from the intercom. "The hell are you guys doing here?"

"Zengus! No time to explain; we're bailing outta here and... how'd you get over here? We heard you were off on other maneuvers."

"Kaitlinn called me back for some kinda emergency at this spot."

"Yeah, that would be us."

"Hah, can't wait to hear this story."

"Tell you on the way. We've got a fix on Cataclysm, and we're beelining for it now."

"Cataclysm? Well, alright, strap in!" The engines revved up and the craft rocked as we launched.

"Set coordinates!" Kado bellowed. "Nelson, get up front on the nav!"

The engine noise went from a deep hum to a shrill whine in

seconds, and I braced against the wall when the craft jostled and launched into the air. I made a personal resolution I had to stop flying like this, preferably to stop flying altogether. A pained belch escaped my lips as I wandered to the front.

I grabbed and pulled my way to the cockpit and looked at the navigation. The text on the strange controls didn't appear in English, but my hands flew to controls on the panel like a paperclip to a magnet. In a few seconds, I typed a course onto the nav and heard a beep sound in response.

"Coordinates received," Zengus commented. "That was easy."

"Just don't ask how I did that."

"You got the touch, man; all I need to know."

Kado laid his hands on our shoulders. "Great work."

Zengus asked, "Think Kaitlinn will try to ground us? They aren't too plenty on Hell Hawks these days."

"She's got too much to worry about with the Omegans, and she's already short one Hell Hawk. Now full on to Cataclysm. Nelson, I've got notes from Baudricort on Failsafe. They're scattered but we need to figure out what's going on with it, if there's anything we need to hack or disable. Sooner I know about it the better, OK?"

The text of the P-LAD danced around, but then it focused for me. The notes were from Baudricort, and they talked about controls and listed a diagram of the Cataclysm unit with a reference to an input port. The device was to be inert until the Failsafe was activated. This was how they prevented unauthorized firing of Cataclysm. It wasn't part of the original design, though it was done by the Valkyrie to prevent accidental discharge of Cataclysm.

"Kado, any idea what these controls are?"

He looked at the notes for a few moments, then checked them against his own P-LAD. "This looks familiar. They were developing a new Link around the time the Action split off. People were becoming more resistant to the Audio suggestions, so they developed an internal one that links to the nervous system. It's far more stable and harder to resist. They'd experimented with the Link, and the one used through the headsets, but it was only one method for them. They'd also tried working with the blood, which was more complex, and the earlier version of that. Before the Link was done. There are examples of this happening, and that looks like what they're talking about."

"So the interface is the nervous system?"

"It's in there somewhere. I just don't have all the details. I'll check back through and find whatever she tied it to. If you get any of those inklings you've been getting, please don't be shy."

"Do you think Charista knows about this?"

"I can't be sure. But I say we get this device and figure out a way. Maybe I can circumvent the Failsafe. We won't know until we get there and try. Step on it, Zengus!"

"How long til we get to the Cataclysm spot?"

"From here, at present speed, another three hours. I'm checking the onboard weapons stores, in case we run into trouble. The rate our luck's been going, we're sure to be in for something."

"We got some of Kado's new guns too. Guess we get to see how they work in the real world now." Norg beamed.

Zengus shifted in his seat. "New guns?"

"Yeah, powered by Valentium."

Zengus stared ahead at the landscape that shot past us. "Hmm, that's... even better."

"Hell yeah, it is." Norg slapped Kado's back.

Kado winced and rolled his eyes. "I wasn't looking forward to seeing them in action."

"We can't rightly choose to fight or not all the time. Cheer up. Just maybe we will miss them on the ground."

"First priority is finding and securing Cataclysm. Then contact Llewyn for his status and see where we can help out. If we can activate Cataclysm, we can turn this whole fight right on its side."

Chapter 13 (Ana)

THE CAPITAL STOOD on a large mountain. Cold gray steel walls lined the squared structure, with sheer sides that made any assault on foot pretty much the dumbest idea ever. Nycole's reaction to my suggestion of going through the air to attempt entry made total sense once I saw the place up close. We'd need a Hell Hawk at least, and then we'd have to hack the security algorithm to let them know this wasn't an enemy stolen craft. And that was all before their defenses engaged. I hadn't any idea what those might be, but as much as Charista had done through MODOSNet and the Link, she must've fortified the hell outta this place.

I was surprised there weren't Omegans around trying to break through. Looked like they were still more about the Valentium, for the time. Kaitlinn also gave the Omegans enough hell to have time for a direct Capital assault, I figured. I hoped she was as good at protecting Nelson as she was at drawing Omegans away from the Range and the Capital.

At least, we didn't need all the hacking I'd figured on. Nycole and Dawn worked their magic with some access codes and before long, we slipped inside.

It took a little doing to get through security, even with psycho research killer Dawn with us. She and Nycole tried emergency beacons, and Lebabolis security authenticated finally our access.

I wondered why they had all that security, but they couldn't find it to spare any tech or resources for their troops in the field. The thought of troops I'd seen and fought along with, some I'd buried, all of whom could've been helped with just some of the weapons and gear that was hoarded around here sent me fuming.

Charista met us at the entrance while we watched the teams seal the entrance up tight.

"What in the world are you doing here?"

Her arms were folded, a stern scowl on her face. That was it, her only greeting to the group and one of the two people with whom she agreed to have Cataclysm delivered to her. It really pissed me off how even now that we were on the same side, she still eyed me like a disapproving parent. After days of walking, eating very little and exhaustion in general, I was surprised at how much resistance I mustered as I kept my hands from clutching her throat right then.

"The Omegans shot us down, and we bailed," I retorted. "Oh, and somebody blew up our Hell Hawk. Don't suppose you know about that?"

Her eyes seethed and she searched for a nasty reply, but her eyes found Nycole and her glance changed quick. It was a brief flicker, and Nycole narrowed hers in some kind of unspoken conversation. I swallowed hard. Nycole gave Charista a knowing smirk in return.

Charista watched me again for a few seconds, then grabbed a small comm from her side. "Of course not. Why would I destroy one of my own officers? Why didn't you check in with Kaitlinn or Jason? They could've helped."

"We might've hit an Omegan patrol before we even got near friendlies."

Charista's eyes darted about us in a visual inventory. "Nelson. He was with you. He didn't—"

"Not so we know. It's tough getting info when your comms are busted."

I thought about the other group we'd seen, the Guard, and why Charista never mentioned 'em. It was like pulling teeth, getting what we even did from Dawn. I kept my mouth shut on that one

135

and hoped Dawn wasn't feeling too generous with the info sharing. *Nice work, Ana. I bet Baudricort would be proud.* The longer I played this game, the easier it got.

"I told them about your ships, ma'am," Dawn said.

Charista said, "Oh? Yes, that's right."

Charista's face twisted as if stung on the heel by an insect. She shrugged the irritation off. "Whatever brought you here, it's time we get on with our primary objective." She spoke a few words into the comm then met my eyes again, this time with a small smirk. "I've notified Harkson. You and Dawn will push on to Cataclysm, and we've got some more... tools for you."

"What about Nelson? Isn't he a crucial part of this too?"

"Nelson, for our purposes, is lost for now. We can't afford to wait anymore, I'm afraid. There's no guarantee he hasn't ended up with the Omegans either."

Dawn stepped up toward my side. "The transports, commander?"

Charista beckoned us over to a MODOSNet terminal, where she tapped controls until diagrams of ships appeared. They were slender and sleek, and nothing like I'd seen. They were longer and skinnier than Hell Hawks. They sure looked fast. Their surface looked seamless, one continual piece of dark shiny metal. Treg stood next to me, his face blank. Wherever these ships were stored and however they came about, the average Warrior Product knew zip about 'em.

"These were in development around the time the Action first broke from Lebabolis. Not even Baudricort knew about them. I'm willing to bet they'll make it."

"You couldn't have brought these around sooner? You realize how many troops are getting killed out there, including your own gray bands?"

"This war got messy fast. Problem is we don't have an unlimited supply of these transport ships. In fact, they're rather short in number. I'm afraid they aren't good for direct assaults. Troops in the field are better off with the Hell Hawks."

"Well, how about letting loose with your garrison?"

"We have to keep enough for the rear guard. This place is our last resort, and we'll defend it to the last."

"Well, now that you're sharing a small piece of your plan, how about letting us in on the rest?"

"It's quite simple, Worker Product. We get Cataclysm and turn it on the Omegans, then that ends them. I can thank Kaitlinn and Jason's regiments for keeping the Omegans occupied until then."

Treg flipped his fingers through the stats on the ships while I took a seat next to Charista. "How's the Pox treatment going?"

"Better than expected." She tapped away on the console, then stopped. "Ana, your brother made it through."

She said the words like she'd read the inventory for a food supply. An excited gasp escaped my lips.

Had I done it?

Was it true?

I choked back a sob at the thought, of Varrick healthy. And now it wasn't just an idea anymore. I felt Treg's arm on my shoulder, and it took me a minute before I answered. "I want to see him."

The terminal sounded with a few beeps, and the symbol of the Valkyrie passed the screen. "In good time. I need to show you part of the gear we'll be supplying you with."

Two soldiers wheeled in a large box that reminded me a lot of the Caches. The cover gleamed a little in the light, black metal with silver trim along the sides. Charista looked at the box as if it were one of her children. "This is the container for Cataclysm. It's very important you place it in here as soon as you get it. Please use extreme care when handling Cataclysm. Any attempts to move or shake it could set it off, so please do not mess this up. I'd rather you had someone like Kado there with you, but there isn't time for a proper outfitting."

"We've handled Valentium runs before; we know about delicate, lady." Treg scoffed.

"I won't debate the safety risks. Just do this as part of our agreement, understand?" Her eyes were fixed on me the whole time, and they narrowed when she mentioned the agreement, as if a verbal slap to my face.

She pulled up several videos on the screen of battles between Lebabolis and the Omegans. At first I thought it was a feed of some of the fighting we'd been into, but faces passed the screen and at one point I recognized Baudricort! The uniforms for Lebabolis looked different, older. Smoke billowed about the soldiers who charged around and fired on each other. In the middle of it was one woman, the Valkyrie. A chill ran through me when I realized why she was familiar. During my Verge, she was the one I had seen who led troops into battle.

The clips showed a force of Omegans in a fight inside the borders of Lebabolis. The Valkyrie stepped about the field, shoulders broad and her head fixed on the scene like a hawk that regarded its prey with serene but laser like focus. She pointed and waved her arms about, directing her troops. They watched her and obeyed with no hesitation. She was calm, cool, even in the sea of destruction around her. I heard the voice who'd spoken to me say, "Across distances I've led you. With valor, strength and victory I've fed you. All evil in this world will dread you."

Charista's face changed. Her scowl softened, and her eyes were stained with a mix of worry and regret. "Years ago the Omegans damaged the borders to Lebabolis and moved pretty far into the Sectors." She eyed me. "We never had time to overhaul them; we were too busy with building back people and infrastructure."

She kept talking, but then I lost all attention to her when another clip played on screen.

"Our army was well trained, but they were overrun. People were in a panic. Worker Products, and Intellectuals especially, aren't accustomed to shows of force and having to defend themselves. They needed something... someone to lead them. The Valkyrie led our troops, but they also stood as a reminder that while we benefit from technology, the old ways are still with us and are always reliable."

I said, "I heard the bedtime stories about her. She and her forces held the Omegans off until Cataclysm finished the job. And you killed her for it."

Charista's eyebrows arched. "Is that what you think of me? You think I'd take our greatest warrior ever and terminate her?"

"See no reason to doubt it."

Charista shook her head. "You haven't heard all of the story. The Valkyrie wanted to break Lebabolis apart, Ana. Harkson, the Coursons and I wanted to retain order."

"You mean slavery."

"I mean progress. Freedom can't exist as anarchy. Without order, the weak fall; they always have. The Valkyrie wouldn't listen to me or the Coursons. She also had the army on her side, so she was too dangerous to be left alone. I had to stand up to her, for the good of the people."

Charista's face clenched. I wasn't sure what happened to her, but she looked like she was in pain telling this story, as if she was being tortured. The usual hard glare I'd known her for was gone, and she looked more like a frightened animal in a trap.

"The Valkyrie was our best and last hope against stopping the Omegans before we had Cataclysm. She had the attention and respect of Lebabolis. But that power went to her head, and she had to be stopped. She tried to shut down our facilities, but it ended up getting more people injured in the process. We just weren't safe anymore with her around. She wanted freedom for all Products, but some of us weren't convinced the Omegans were really gone. And we had no stability without order. If we were left to our own, things would have gone back to people destroying each other. Our system was tough, but in a world close to its end, sometimes order must come before freedom. Now I want to show you where you came from, Ana, because we need you. We need you and the Action, and you need us, even if you don't realize it yet.

"Ana, I'm desperate to stop the Omegans and we need your help. There, I said it." She slid her fingers and moved them briskly about the controls. The screens switched to Product files and histories, and before I knew it, there was mine. My entire existence reduced to a single screen. The only thing that was blank was the parents. Those two fields were cleared out.

"Your records have always been like this. I assume

Baudricort wanted secrecy for you, like some of the others who fled to the Action. We eliminated his access for this once we learned what he had done, but not before he damaged a lot of records."

I thought back to his eyes as he lay there dying in my arms. Was he just sorry because he knew he was dying? No, my heart never accepted that. He got people out. That wasn't Baudricort. Was it?

Everything in me figured he wanted me protected by doing this. All of us in the Action knew we were doomed for Realignment if we got caught.

"As I told you, the Action started out as training for our new army. We wanted to resurrect the Valkyrie. Once we learned the Omegans were assembling for another invasion, we knew time was short. Preparing Radomet takes too long, and we needed people who could be made ready much sooner."

The screen switched back to another profile record. I hadn't seen this one before, but a glimpse of the face really resonated with me. It was the face of the woman I had in the Verge, the one on the videos.

"The Valkyrie?" I asked.

"Her name was Petra." Her voice trembled just saying the name. The ember of emotion smoldering in Charista's voice stunned me. It was the first time I heard anything from her other than the cold commanding tone that greeted me on the MODOSNet updates, or Product training speeches or even the dealings we had with her as part of the Action. We'd joked that her heart was just a mechanical device where emotion was as absent as water in a desert. To us she was a Radomet with well-hidden mechanical parts.

But before I could ask about anything else, she continued. "Petra was the Valkyrie. We grew up together, two Warrior Products and friends. She led the army to victory against the Omegans. She was our protectress. I rose up too, but with the regular military. In time I had my own command. But the Valkyrie oversaw the Guard and the true elite of the Lebabolis strength." She strained when she said the word 'elite', as if it bothered her that it hadn't been applied to her or who she commanded."

Charista continued, "When a majority agreed we needed stronger controls, tighter security, Petra resisted. She refused to let Lebabolis go the way they were. She never understood the benefit of order for moving ahead. She insisted on freedom, but we'd seen the Outlands. That's no more than chaos. A lot of people joined her; she had a lot of supporters. Some people can't handle that kind of power. She became rash, reckless. We had a foothold of civilization in this world, and it soon became clear she would only jeopardize that."

"But then why the torture and Realignment?"

"Only for order. People need direction and purpose. You think the Outlands are less harsh than Realignment? I suggest you spend more time out there. All the Outlands offer is blight and a slim chance of survival. You've been out there for a while now; do you really see that place offering anything other than chaos?

"There's more," Charista said and hesitated. She watched me, her brow wrinkled. "Should I continue?"

"I don't know what you're gonna say, so it's up to you."

"Ana, we fought with Petra a lot over what she wanted. Before we stopped her, she went on raids trying to break our system from within. Those raids included attacks on facilities. She was so determined to break up Lebabolis, she lashed out, she and her troops. They stormed facilities, shut down things they could, and in all of this a lot of Lebabolis products were killed. Including, I'm afraid, your mother."

My body went taut at this. The Valkyrie killed Lebabolis products? But there it was: Petra blasted production facilities, and I noticed Sector Five, my home sector. And the woman who had my name laid out to rest.

"I don't understand. She was the Protectress. Why would she?"

"Desperation. She lost her mind, Ana. She started out good. I knew her from little and she was the best we had to offer here, but later in her life she became something else. Intentions, however good, can get blurred with time. I'm sorry to be the one to tell you this, and I don't know why Baudricort never did. I suppose he was too embarrassed about his own transgressions and for not taking better care of you."

"Baudricort started this?"

"He was under strict orders from the Coursons to develop a weapon. He architected Cataclysm to stop the Omegans."

As she talked, Charista's expression softened. I thought of the nomadic life the Action had, and even this location of the Range didn't really offer much other than shelter. We had no structure, at best a haphazard one from Baudricort's half crazed obsession with rescuing people from the mistake he'd created and given to our world.

"I figured in time, once our reach was further, we could consider more freedom. But I care too much about the citizens of Lebabolis, of which you're still one too, to let them flounder in self destruction." Charista breathed a heavy sigh; her eyes were distant.

The vision of Charista as a child seemed as odd to me as a third arm. I wondered how all this time she hadn't managed to pull a coup and kill Harkson to take command of the Coursons and Lebabolis. If there was anything she wanted and liked and desired, it was power. She gravitated to it like no one else I ever knew.

The more she talked about Petra, the more Petra sounded like Baudricort. Quite strong willed; made me wonder how he would've handled her. "So she was brought in for Realignment?"

"That wasn't an option back then. In fact we never had any other chance to convince or stop her. She broke out with the Guard when word was received a group of Omegans massed near our border, and Petra was never heard from again. We always assumed she was lost."

"So she wanted freedom, but instead of that you lay down an even tighter rein on people. How is that any better?" I asked. "The Valkyrie wanted to return the rule and the decisions to the people. Why isn't that better than keeping people living like cattle, producing like pieces of machinery?"

"In time, there could be more freedom, but we can't consider that with the Omegans at our door. You really think we can drop everything with this army hell bent on raiding and ruining everything we've built to date? Dear Ana, you must consider the world Lebabolis developed in. Chaos was the rule, the strong devoured the weak. To leave any society to that kind of rule would be to just invite more problems among those who couldn't defend themselves. Lebabolis has a mission to establish order, and that's our goal."

I wondered if our plans to live free were really considered part of their deal. But I wasn't about to let that thought slip into Charista's cross hairs.

Charista looked at me with sad eyes. "All I can say is when the Valkyrie was gone, I lost a friend and Lebabolis lost a great asset. We've stumbled down the road of progress, but it doesn't mean we haven't made a lot of great advances.

"But now we need something. We're protecting the future of Lebabolis, but we need help guarding its present. Jason and Kaitlinn command our field troops and the Coalition, and are keeping them at bay, but troops need a rally point. If anything, the Valkyrie taught us that having a champion is what spears soldiers on to win. We want you to be that champion for us."

"Me?"

She nodded. "You've got respect of both the military and the people. You were a Worker Product who burst out and thrived. You even outfought Radomet. You showed how the Product system doesn't always serve the best needs. Ana, we want you to be the Valkyrie. Deliver Cataclysm and lead our attack. We'll have Kaitlinn make the troops ready for you so you can lead them into battle. Llewyn's group is near the Range and he needs help. We need it to be you."

"I don't know, what could I do?"

"What you've been doing, what you've been trained to do, what you've always done... what's in your heart. Show the Omegans that they can't control this world and they won't own us."

143

"But when we have Cataclysm?"

"That's our guarantee. The Valkyrie fought the Omegans to a standstill before Cataclysm finished them last time, and I know you can do it now. The peace will be ensured once we have Cataclysm."

I watched Treg. Leading the attack, the whole attack? How could I be expected to do this? All I had to go on were the words of someone who claimed to be the Valkyrie talking to me in my head.

A few people rounded the corner with a small child. My eyes leapt to them and when I saw Varrick's face, I froze. My throat seized up as if I were about to choke. My eyes brimmed with tears. I felt like I'd been punched in the gut. My breaths came too fast for words. My legs shook, but somehow I stayed on my feet and took an awkward step toward him. I squinted my eyes shut, and the tears dripped over my cheeks unchecked.

"I kept my bargain." Charista stood and watched Varrick as he ran and jumped into my arms.

"Sister!"

I kissed him and rubbed the back of his head, my voice in a full tremble. "Y-you're OK?"

"Uh huh." His voice was bright, like he hadn't recently been sick with a life threatening illness very recently.

My arms snaked around his form and squeezed him tight while my body shook with sobs. I closed my eyelids and let the tears come. I didn't have to be brave, I didn't have to be strong. I felt like I hadn't in many years.

The warmth burst through me like rainfall. My body relaxed, and for a moment I wasn't a leader of troops in the Coalition or even the Action, I wasn't this fearsome soldier, this brutal machine with a Worker Product's heart and a Warrior Product's skill.

And for that moment, I didn't have to be either.

I held my young brother and for just a moment I became a child again too. I let the feeling flow through me. My knees buckled, and I fell to the floor. I opened my eyes and the tears blurred my vision, but I didn't even care.

144

He was OK.

And with me.

I watched his face, his smile, oh that smile I hadn't seen in forever. I exhaled a sob as the weight of what I'd been through, and not knowing how Varrick was, was lifted in an instant. My heart ached as I wondered what to do so that this moment would last always.

In an instant, what I'd been through, what we had left to do, was all worth it. Doubt melted away like ice in sunlight. A warm energy hit me, and I didn't care where it came from, just that it felt like love returning to me as a river that flooded a dry oasis. I blinked back the tears, and my voice shook with all the agony of not having seen Varrick well, or even at all for so many months.

My voice hitched as I spoke. "Oh, my little man. It's good to see you." I hugged him as tight as I could. "What are they doing with you over here?" I took a gulp of air and exhaled into more happy sobs.

"They let us walk but only inside. They say it's safer."

I laughed. It felt more like home, this cold capital, for the first time ever. Even with Nelson and my other friends still away and under attack, I felt a calmness I'd been missing. I quickly regretted that I had to leave. It was mandatory. We had to get back to the front. There was no way I could let those people be out there.

I had no idea what Charista thought of the Valkyrie or that knife that I had. She never asked for it, but I wondered if someday she'd have aimed it at my back.

The sight of Charista so broken up over what happened to her friend, Petra, made me wonder how much war had messed her up too. War made even the hardest one of us crumble, even just a little.

I smiled at the thought of the light now back in my present, with Varrick at my side. And my future had a glimmer now. If I pressed on and finished my deal with Charista, I had a shot at making a real home with my brother.

Chapter 14 (Ana)

I WORKED TO PROCESS everything Charista had said. It was weird how little I'd known about her before. Even more how sad she was about what she said. Maybe we'd underestimated her all this time. I knew I was ready for this all to be over, and now I knew that maybe she was too. Charista always was the figurehead we saw for updates on the Security of Lebabolis, and to have her not only know the Valkyrie but to have grown up with her was strange.

Charista's story reminded me of how much I never had. A family she knew, choices she wanted, and recognition. It seemed so distant, like one of those stories we heard over and over again about the Valkyrie. It felt like she talked about another race of people or country. I never knew anyone who had it even close like that where I grew up.

I'd never heard anything about her and the Valkyrie. The stories I was told were more about inspiration, not on who was whose best friend.

And now she wanted me to lead the charge. I wanted more than anything to get back at the Omegans, but what to do about Cataclysm worried me. Was Duncan right? Was I crazy, giving it to her? I was too tired at that point for any more strategy plans like Baudricort.

I wished Nelson was here, but I had to think he was safer with

Kaitlinn or one of the Guard tribes for then. I'd figure out a way to get him back to his time. Kado had to have something.

The sweeping ceilings and ramps of the Capital's interior led lower below the surface into the mountain. The lighting cast a faded glow everywhere. Charista wanted me to meet with Harkson, and for once I was happier to meet with him after her mood changed so much. I needed a father figure, and as much as I hadn't wanted it to be Harkson, he was the closest thing I had to that here.

While people were locked in at the Capital, they were allowed time for meals and light exercise, as long as shifts were kept. A group always had to be ready for exterior defense and monitoring of the proximity alarms too.

The Capital facility was large over ground and it had a network beneath for quarters. They took their time and built a pretty solid fortress, or at least they had their Products do it for them. The sight of the detailed structures, reinforced walls, quarters, food ration supplies, just got me angrier than I'd ever thought it would make me. I thought about Products I knew, grew up around, and lived with. They suffered and in some cases died so places like this were built. It made that deal I had with Charista as tough to take as the first day we made it.

Some people brushed past me as I walked toward one of the great dining halls. The room was filled with the low roar of people stuffing their faces. I watched the loyal Products, those who either couldn't or wouldn't break and go with the Action, feeding themselves. Their faces filled with contentment of their reward received. I shook my head at the thought that after this was over, they'd just go back to their lives of slavery, doing whatever their master wanted of them. Then I wondered, what if this didn't end for them, if this was where it ended for all of us among the living?

I was about to leave the room when I heard a younger man's voice call out, "Ana!"

A group of products at a nearby table watched me. One man stood, a grin from ear to ear. I stepped toward him. The gentle roar of the crowd eating enveloped us. "Is that really you?"

I searched his face, but nothing in it was familiar. Why hadn't I recognized this guy when he knew me? I'd eaten, but still hadn't gotten any sleep; that must've been it.

He let out a small chuckle. "Haven't seen you since Instruction!"

Then I remembered.

Watson.

Watson was a fellow Worker Product from the same housing unit. He knew me, Treg, Norg and the rest of the Circle well. He'd helped my adopted parents with Varrick on occasion in our housing unit, and if I'd have stayed we would have been fellow facility workers for sure.

"I'll be damned. I wondered what happened to you since I took off." I laughed.

"We heard about that break. Saw you a few times on the MODOSNet updates, until that crash anyway. We thought you died."

"Nah, it was close but we made it."

"You seen Varrick?"

I nodded and brushed a hand quick past one eye. "Yeah, he looks great."

"They've been running people through this contraption since we got here. Say they cured a good thousand people of Pox already."

"Good, that was part of our deal with 'em."

"Treg still with you?"

"Yeah, he's here too. They're sending us on a mission."

"Mission? What's with the outfit?"

"Well, the Action and Lebabolis formed the Coalition—"

"Oh, that's right. How could I forget? You're a big bad Warrior Product now. How'd you even get over on them?"

"Guess they liked how I took care of myself in a fight. So who else is here with you?"

"Oh, a few folks from our Sector, but they kinda mixed us together now. We're grouped by Product."

"What do they have you doing here?"

"Oh, food and exercise mostly. Gets boring a lot these past

few months. But some of us are loading up a stash of Valentium. It's slow, and that job has been the same for a while. Don't matter much; I'd rather have something to do."

"Loading Valentium? What for?"

"I suspect it's for resupplying regiments. They gotta be running on empty, much as we see them fighting on MODOSNet."

"I didn't realize they still sent out MODOSNet updates here."

"Oh, hell yeah. Too many of us to jabber to all at once. They give us the latest. We saw that fight in the Crater. They have us hooked in when we aren't on extra duties."

"What kind of extra duties?"

"Oh, like running maintenance, monitoring the perimeter. Kolb over there's the one who caught y'all on your entry beacon in fact. Whatever they got, it's way more boring than facility work. But you don't know about that, now, do you? Kolb heard a few officers talking the other day about some big move that was going down. Something about a Range."

My gut froze up tight at the word, and I thought of our people still out there. They never felt more like mine at that point, and I was terrified they were walking into a place they'd be stuck in.

"Well, just keep your head down, Wats. I may not see you again before they send us."

"Look at you. You know we heard what happened on your Exodus breakout." His eyes beamed. "That was damned brave."

"Aww, well, things get blown up more after they're passed around through a few people."

"Don't sound blown up to me. In fact, Treg told me about it."

My throat clenched at the memory and the sight of myself through Wats' eyes, and I had to leave at that. "Nice seeing you again, Wats. Just take care of yourself, and I'll pass back any word I can."

"Sounds good. Look, we've been thinking. If you're going to make the Range, we want to come. Can you take a few of us with you?"

"How the hell can we do that? I'm pretty sure you'll be

noticed, and they won't take too kindly to something like that."

"Anything, just... I'm getting real bad feelings about this."

"I know. I can tell you, if I have anything to say about it, this war is gonna come to an end pretty damned soon."

"I'm holding you to that."

"Well, good then." I smirked. "Take care of yourself, Wats!"

I needed more time for my thoughts, so I walked further into the halls of the Capital until I ended up in the hangar and watched the sleek transport ships Dawn had gone on about. There they were, five of them. They looked nothing like the Hell Hawks. These were long and slender, and there were very few guns on the outside. They'd better be pretty damned fast, because about all they'd be good for in a fight is a battering ram, or just a target for Omegan gunners. One of the ships was being loaded with Valentium, like Wats had said. Were they supplying troops? Or was it for a run separate from the Cataclysm one?

It had to be. Why the hell would we carry that kinda load with us that far?

I ran my hand over the smooth metal of one of the craft wings when the voice returned to me.

She's lying, you know.

+What do you mean?+

The Valkyrie. She's right about the Valkyrie, but she knows just what happened to her. And she's not dead. Not yet, anyway.

+What makes you so sure?+

Because I'm her.

I exhaled in a gasp. A painful chill arrowed through me, and I clutched my sides in a deep shiver. The techs working on the craft glanced my way, but I just waved them off. The whole time I'd been talking with her, the killer of my mother?

I spun around and plodded back out of the hangar.

+You're Petra?+

Yes.

My whole body jerked upright as if I were a piece of rope pulled taut. I'd been talking with her... her.

150

+Is she wrong about you killing my mother, then?+

She paused for a long while. *I don't know.*

+Oh, well, you have no idea what I've been through, what I'm going through now, what I'll always go through over this. I don't know who to believe, but I'm thinking I'd be a lot more peaceful without you, so let me know where you are and I'll make sure I end your body wherever it is and whatever state it's in.+

Ana, please, hear me out.

+Why the hell should I even listen to you at all? I need answers; I want to know why this happened!+

What I do know, as dangerous as you think I am, Charista is a thousand times worse.

+I don't care. Why don't you leave me the hell alone?+

I want to help you.

+Help me do what?+

Save your people, your brother, Nelson.

+How?+

Ana, I'm talking about what Charista said, her plan for you to get Cataclysm. Let me help you.

+Why should I?+

Because I once swore to protect Lebabolis and I failed. I want to do what I always set out to do but wasn't strong enough to accomplish because of my pride. I know I don't deserve your attention or help, and I certainly don't deserve your forgiveness. I've tortured myself far longer than you ever could, trust me.

+At least tell me how you're communicating with me all this time. Are you using the Link?+

I am.

+How?+

They set it up so well, they didn't realize someone with enough ability could use it to send their own messages out.

+If you're here at the Capital, or anywhere to know where I'm at, why haven't you just come to me?+

I can't; they took that from me.

+What do you mean, took that from you?+

*They took my physical freedom when they made me into a

Radomet.*

+You're a—how did that happen?+

It was the only way. I was scheduled for Realignment—

+Charista said it wasn't invented at the time.+

Oh, it was. Baudricort was ingenious and quick. We had it around the time we had Cataclysm. They took my troops away and told me they were gassed. They didn't want to take any chances of making them Radomet; they were afraid they would overpower the system and break the coding. They could've busted out of the holding and made a break for it. They wanted them taken care of fast and clean. For me they wanted to experiment and clone me, using their tech to make an army of mindless drones. I was to be the template, kept locked away and duplicated to keep their supply of warriors filled. But I was saved at the last moment by a friend. Instead, I was sent for Radomet conversion. They completed everything except the neural break, which allowed me to communicate like this.

+Why can't you just get out of there; what are you doing around?+

I'm only one person, and I'm trapped. I can't leave the Capital. If my troops were around, I'd have a shot. But instead I've been biding my time. Lebabolis is too powerful. Now with the Omegans at their door it might be easier for me to make a stand.

My head ached with this. Charista was only interested in keeping things to herself. She never stopped her schemes, even toward those who were supposed to be her allies. She wanted control. But the Valkyrie would've known about the Omegans and how to defeat 'em. Charista wasn't afraid of the Valkyrie destroying the Omegans. She was just afraid she wouldn't be able to control the Valkyrie ever.

You must be very careful and think again about her. She's got no interest in defeating the Omegans. I haven't been able to prove it and the Coursons wouldn't accept it, but I know she's worked out some kind of deal. We fought them to a near standstill and Cataclysm turned them back for years, but I knew just as she did that they'd come back one day. She needed a bargaining chip so they'd agree to give Lebabolis their own land and exist side by side. Two enemies in a truce, however unstable.

+How long have you been like this?+

I stopped counting at around five years, so it's anybody's guess now.

+I've got news for you about the Guard; they aren't gone. At least, not Duncan and his group.+

Wha- how do you know that name?

+Because he's alive, along with your troops. I've seen them.+

What?

+The Guard? I've seen 'em, well some of 'em.+

Really, where?

+When we came through a Sector, they attacked a group of Omegans testing a Disruptor. They were poorly armed, and they turned the Omegans back.+

Where?

+In the wilderness, about a day's walk from the capital. They overpowered an Omegan patrol.+

The voice shuddered. *Unbelievable. They live. So they've joined you.*

+No, not at all.+

Why not?

+I tried, but you wouldn't recognize them. They aren't what you remember. They were more interested in surviving than a fight.+

No, that cannot be. They swore to fight and die with me.

+And now they think you're dead, and their own country turned them away to let them scrap like rodents. Why should they still care about anything?+

They pledged to stand with me and a country, and were cast aside. You can convince them to return.

+I tried but it was a clear no.+

Did you show them the knife?

+Yes, but they think it was stolen.+

What about the beacon?

+What beacon?+

The knife. Built into the handle is a beacon. Only the Valkyrie would know how to activate it.

+Yeah, so what do I do then?+ I pulled out the knife and flipped it around. The raised sigil pressed into my palm.

Rotate the handle to the left until you hear a click. Then push the emblem on the handle. That does it.

I followed her instructions. The handle took a little work but it finally budged, and when I pressed the sigil I heard two high pitch beeps, then nothing."

+So that's it?+

Yes.

+But wouldn't Charista have known about that?+

No, that was never shown to her. Your friend Baudricort—

+You mean my father.+

Yes, of course, your father Baudricort set that beacon up.

+But how do you even know they're monitoring it? They had no real weapons or tech I saw and smelled like they'd been living outdoors for the past ten years.+

When you're short on options your number one has to be hope.

+Now you're sounding like me.+ I clutched the handle in my hand again. I felt it warm up beneath my fingers. +So is this thing sending now?+

Yes, it will continue to unless you shut it off.

+How do I do that, anyway? In case someone we don't like is listening too.+

Repeat the process, but don't do it until you're in their presence. That's your proof that you know me.

+It's a long shot.+

You have to try again, Ana. You can do it.

+I don't even know where to find them.+

Start by looking due west from Sector Two in the Outlands. There once was a settlement there, thirteen miles from the Lebabolis border.

+It's been more than twenty years. What makes you sure they're so intact? That group I saw coulda been all of 'em. The Outlands aren't the best place to rough it on your own.+

154

You must try, Ana. Remember, I saw you when you made the Verge jump all those centuries back.

+You're the one who called out to me?+

I was. And I saw you do something amazing for someone who was only supposed to be a Worker Product. With no direction, you grabbed control of the situation you were thrust into and made that leap. Even Warrior Products get hesitant at times, but not you. You're a soldier, and whoever trained you did their job well. You completed the mission and helped many people. But now people need you again. Your friends need you. You can't let Charista get her hands on Cataclysm. It's too dangerous for anyone to have. So search, use the beacons, figure it out. It's what you've done, what you've always done.

+What do I say to 'em? They weren't even interested at all; they just wanted to get away.+

Tell them this: Across distances I've led you—with valor, strength and victory I've fed you. All the evil of the world will dread you.

+What is that?+

The Valkyrie pledge. Every member of the Guard knows it. In fact it was so volatile that when Lebabolis disbanded the Guard and sent me for Realignment that code was rendered illegal. If they hear someone speak it, that should give them enough of a push.

+So you worked with Baudricort. My father?+

There was a pause. *Yes, I knew him very well. He can help you.*

+I'm afraid not. He's dead.+

The voice gasped and shuddered. When she spoke again, her voice was stained with emotion. *How did it happen?*

+It's still a mystery. He was killed by a bomb at one of our bases, but we never found who did it.+

Her voice trembled more. *He believed in what I did, what I still do, with every breath I have in my body, in this mechanical shell they've locked me in. Without safety and strength, evil will win. Find the Guard, Ana. Repeat what I said.*

+But their deal to cure Varrick and the rest depends on me

finding Cataclysm.+

You made a promise with someone incapable of doing so, I'm afraid.

+But they cured Varrick! I saw him.+

Be careful. I'm an expert on dealing with Charista, and look where it's gotten me. Just remember, things aren't always what they seem.

+I had no choice.+

I know. But now you do. If you don't stop Charista, there won't be much of anything or anyone else left to save, my dear. Be careful. Charista has eyes everywhere, and don't think she's not trying to get into your mind via the Link.

+And the Omegans? Can we stop them at all?+

They want something, plain and simple. Find Cataclysm, and you'll have what they and everyone else who wants power desires.

+Power?+

Control, but power too. And the Guard will give you the edge to find it and defend it if they get the chance, if you show them they can strike back over what was taken from them.

+Even if I do this, and they go along and we somehow manage to turn back the Omegans, what about Charista? She'll still be in power, she'll still have the ability to develop, and she'll come up with something else before long.+

First stop the immediate threat. The Omegans will drain the world for resources before they leave. There'll be no stopping them just yet either. If they do, this planet will no longer be habitable. Ana, your list of enemies is growing, you better add to your collection of friends. If you get to Cataclysm first, Baudricort has something there for you.

+Oh?+

Yes, but you must get to the device to see it. Just don't let other people know about me and our Link at the Capital. They don't like those who are different, and you don't want Charista to get any more plans for you than she already has.

Chapter 15 (Nelson)

AFTER A BLISTERING FLIGHT across miles and miles of jagged terrain, over and around mountains like some sort of extended rugged machine test, we arrived at the location for Cataclysm. The mountains stared back at us like an angry pack of lions. We glided past a collection of boulders, scattered around like pieces of popcorn spilled on a floor. Our ship weaved slow and steady toward the taller mountains, where my Pull was so strong that I shook.

I clutched the armrests of my seat and took several deep breaths. I hoped getting Cataclysm also meant these feelings would finally stop.

We topped a few more grassy hills and saw a flatland, still with random boulders and rocks, but a level path that slowly arched up to the mountains appeared in front of us. I felt this tug in one direction. It wasn't super strong, but it was enough that if we moved a different way I felt unbelievably nauseous. I noticed a reach of boulders and some reddish soil, and I felt the direction was the right one to go, so I pointed Zengus to where my "feeling" showed me.

Reilly rode next to me in the comm seat. He was pretty brawny, and among Norg and Zengus, that really said something. He'd been part of the group with Kaitlinn that was supposed to haul us back with her in force. Once Zengus explained things about our situation better though, Reilly went along. His glasses lay across his nose, and he looked on me with a smirk that he held for most people. He was in maintenance, but it was pretty clear if things got physical, Reilly was one of the guys who'd be throwing down early.

We touched down near a cave that jutted out from the side of one mountain like a hungry mouth. The air right inside the entrance was damp. I wiped the moisture that collected on my forehead. Kado ran a scan for signs from any other forces but found nothing. We unloaded, grabbed torches and weapons and headed inside. A dank moist air greeted us on the way in, with a rotting smell of a place that had no ventilation ever. A snake slithered past us into the darkness.

"You never mentioned snakes," Kado muttered.

I shot him a glare. "What am I, a tour guide?"

"Given everything that's happened, I'd expect you know a lot about this place, more than you may even realize."

"You should know by now, it doesn't work like that for me."

The ground was rocky and slippery, and more than a few times one of us slid to the ground in the near darkness. We took slow steps on the soft ground.

"Still got those feelings, Nelson?" asked Norg.

"Stronger than ever. Ready for this to be over. It's weird but I'm walking right where I'm pulled, if that makes any sense."

"As much as anything. I posted Reilly by the entrance of the cave for a sentry. Let's keep an eye out; I don't want us wandering off where we might get stuck."

"Of course."

Zengus lifted his light above and lit up the ceiling, and its jagged slopes of rock pressed into each other in crooked and broken arches.

Zengus pointed at the fractured rocks. "Looks like there's been a few cave-ins here over time. We used to look around in caves like this back at my Sector. Watch your surroundings, case we need to bail fast. Everybody remember your bearings and the way out. It's real easy to get spun around in here if you're not careful."

"Eyes out," Kado murmured as he tapped away on his P-LAD. "I'm scanning the area. Let's go slow here; we got a big prize to haul in. Don't want to waste time looking where we shouldn't."

The cave was filled with silence other than the small sounds we made as we talked on occasion and padded our feet over the unstable ground. I remembered my trip with Ana out of Sector Five in the beginning of all this, when she saved me from having my mind altered and destroyed. I felt another Pull but kept it in check, even though it still shot up to the surface now and then.

The deeper we went, the moister the air got. The Pull got even stronger too, so I knew we were right on target. I walked through a wall of cold air. The chill it sent up the back of my neck stopped me quick. The Pull moved to my throat, and I managed a startled cough.

"You alright?" Zengus asked.

"We're close. Real close. We should even stop and check here; this may be it."

The path widened, and a ledge formed out of the rock off to our right. We fanned out and looked around. The dim light from our torches threw a lot of shadows around, and showed just piles of rock and dirt, with a makeshift path through it all. I scanned my eyes and strained for any more details than my eyes gave me right then. My view settled on one section of rubble and passed over it before I felt myself pulled back there.

I looked off somewhere else again, but my head jerked back as if invisible hands directed it back to the same place. Before long I pointed right at the spot. "There it is."

A smooth ledge jutted out from the floor of the cave up four feet, a wall of rock that flowed up to a platform. Loose boulders were placed all around to make it semi-visible to anyone who wasn't looking right at it.

Norg and Zengus snaked from behind me and stood, their thighs pressed against the ledge. They slid rocks and other rubble away from the spot until they revealed a large crate. I shone my torch on it. The case was covered with black soot and grime, but the light found a few glimmers of metal. It had some markings I didn't recognize; there was too much grime on it.

The center of the top part had a larger reflective surface, and I made out the crossed blade and bolt of the Valkyrie.

"Paydirt," Norg muttered.

I grasped the P-LAD in the darkness and activated it. I pulled the notes up on the screen. The letters stared at me in their original state, and after a few minutes they rearranged to form letters and words I understood. Diagrams amid the notes explained how to open the crate, so I directed the others on unlocking it.

I watched and called out details that flowed from my uncomprehending eyes to my brain and out through my mouth. Part of my mind watched the whole scene as if it were some kind of movie. After a few minutes the case was open. For all I'd heard about this device, it looked average to me. I don't know what I'd expected; anything more elaborate than this. Several circuit boards and a swirl of wires with switches. The whole thing emitted a bluish glow. It looked old, even by this time's standards. I wondered if it even worked anymore. It was a lot smaller than I'd thought, for a machine that caused so much destruction.

Norg grunted. "So now what?"

"What do you mean?" asked Kado.

"Let me tell you now what." Zengus' pulse rifle activated and made me jump; it was the only sound we heard in the cave. "I suggest you get to hauling that thing out and hand it over to me good and fast."

"What're you doing, man?" Norg's face was twisted in confusion.

I traded confused glances with Kado. He reached a hand toward Zengus and flinched when Zengus swung his rifle to Kado in response.

"Um, Zengus, what's going on?"

"All that needs to be, Intellectual Product. All you need to know is I made my own deal out of this whole situation. See, you're going at this the wrong way, searching and gunning and fighting for what? Stopping the Omegans? Still think they're out to get us? Why don't you consider just how easy it's been for them, and then let me tell you why. You've got the wrong information on them. We're not their enemies. We're their slaves."

"What?"

"You heard me."

"Zengus, what makes you even think that?"

"I got a good dosage on one of my raids I flew up in Jason's regiment. They've been pulling more of us out to help with the Omegan gathering humans up."

"Gathering humans?" Kado waved his arms about. "Zengus, this is ridiculous. You know Charista's been sending suggestions through the Link for years now. I think your imagination has just gotten away from you."

Zengus sneered. "Wrong again, brain child. You've been fed the same story like most people, even Baudricort. Poor bastard never even realized he'd been helping keep this little scenario going, all those years working on the Link and programming us like the onboard systems of a Hell Hawk."

I asked, "But the way you say it, not just the Omegans were in on this. If they're pulling people to help as you say, someone else in Lebabolis knew."

"Charista." Zengus scoffed as if the effort of saying her name was beneath him, like it was some secret we were all supposed to know.

I felt my knees wobble beneath me, and I steadied myself against the wall of the cave.

Zengus laughed and shook his head in pity toward us. "Y'all still thinking I'm crazy; well, let me just explain it better. We're generations into a gigantic farming experiment."

"Farming for what, Valentium?"

"Us, fool. Us. We're the crop."

"What?"

"You heard me. Centuries ago, the human race were reduced to a stash of embryonic cells in storage. Seems the powers that were back then made arrangements in case the shit royally hit the fan. And when it did, they had their backup plan. Only they didn't realize just how bad shit would get, so thousands of these

161

embryonic hosts sat and stayed. Until another race came along, the Omegans. They weren't even looking for us. They stopped over to drain this planet and thought we'd make good helpers for that before they turned this whole place into dust."

"You're telling me that they reconstituted an entire race? Why?"

"That ain't for me to even begin to determine, brain child. How's about you, Mr. Author? You got any ideas why this all happened?"

The idea of the Omegans and what they did hadn't entered my mind one bit. "No. I'm at a loss. I always figured we'd be wiped out in a nuclear war. But I've no other idea."

"So we'll just have to wait for the book, I suppose. If you live long enough to finish it." Zengus sneered.

Sloshing footsteps grew louder in the corridor behind Zengus until Reilly's face was framed in the dim light, his pulse rifle pointed, the tip glowing and ready. I watched how he regarded Zengus, and it told me whose side he was on.

Zengus nodded, then pointed to the case. "So let's move this thing on out."

"I ain't moving jack nowhere," Norg muttered. "You better shoot me now and save us all the trouble."

"Norg, what would we do without that badass mean you pull off so well?" Zengus nodded to Reilly, who jammed a metallic claw in Norg's arm. The claw came to life with a shrill tone and the sound of metallic gears clinking. "Gotta hand it to those Omegans, they brought all this kind of tech to us for their experiment. We've added tweaks, but I bet it's nothing like theirs."

Norg's body shook in violent convulsions. He took labored breaths as saliva shot from his mouth. This went on for a few minutes, and his eyes shut tight. When he opened them they emitted a pale blue glow.

"And now we have our own drone product." Zengus admired their handiwork for a few moments. There was Norg, in body anyway. But it was pretty clear from his face that he wasn't there. Even the crinkled lines on his brow from his frowns were gone, and his eyes were blank aside from their new hue.

"What the hell did you do to him?" I asked.

"Oh, just a little temporary sedative to make him less interested in being an asshole. Should keep him docile til we can make it permanent back at the Capital. Now, Nelson, Kado, put those puny ass arms to use and help Norg carry this thing out."

I folded my arms. "Why the hell should I listen to you, traitor?"

Zengus laughed as Reilly readied another claw device. "Xander, much as I'd like to kill you, there are plenty of people on the Omegan side as well who'd just love to get a closer look at you. Think I'd deprive them of the pleasure? Hell, no!"

"Save your mind, Nelson. There are other alternatives here. Let's wait it out," Kado whispered.

Norg's body twisted like a piece of machinery and he grasped the handles on the edge of the box and lifted. Once Kado and I grasped and pulled the box came free. My arms got sore in a few minutes.

We slowly walked back down the path way with Zengus and Reilly behind us.

"So the package we'd been talking about and wondering what it was. All this time, it's us. We're not joining up to fight the Omegans; we're being handed over to them."

"How did I let this go this far this long?" Kado's voice was as broken as the expression on his face.

I said, "It's ok, don't beat yourself up. At least Ana wasn't here for this."

Kado eyed me. "She's probably dead, you know."

"No, Kado. I feel it," I said.

"How can you even—wait, you feel it? Like the Pull?"

"Yep." I nodded and smiled at Kado.

Kado asked, "What about the Pull for Cataclysm?"

"That's settled for now," I said.

Kado watched me for a moment then said, "So Zengus, since you have us cornered and will be delivering your package soon, why not tell us more?"

Zengus scoffed. "In case you get free? Hah, not gonna happen. I've contacted an Omegan regiment, and they'll be here within the hour. Your days of running and planning all over this place are over, Xander."

I asked, "Then how about you tell me what I've got in store? Least you can do for me leading you here to begin with."

Zengus said, "As soon as our other inside person is in position, you'll be brought over to the Omegans for processing. They're interested in collecting their experiment and reining it back in. They wanted humans as a worker force, but they also gave them some of their tools and tech, showed them how it worked. And we learned fast, learned how to make a lot of weapons that destroyed things. They kept us going for a long time doing that. But something happened they never expected. Humans developed. We organized and created a society. We were self-aware, and not just these obedient workers anymore. We thought for ourselves and wanted more than they wanted us to have. All the skills left in the species when it was dormant came back to life. The Omegans who were watching over the Colony were way outnumbered."

Kado asked, "So they managed to form Lebabolis the country?"

Zengus said, "Yeah, did plenty. The Valentium they were mining for, they kept on doing that. They made their deliveries to the Omegans. They made a peaceful offer. But things developed and got more involved. Then Lebabolis determined it wasn't ready to keep delivering to their masters. They wanted their own and so they shut the Omegans off and, well, it didn't go so well."

"So all this time, Charista has been part of this experiment too?" I asked.

"Yes," Zengus said.

"And she's never said anything about it?" I asked.

Zengus said, "She had plans to break free; she figured that she could've. The Valkyrie gave her hope, and especially, having Cataclysm, it was a clear option that she could shut them down forever."

Kado asked, "What made her think they'd just let her go like that?"

Zengus said, "Can't say. People have so much power they forget who they are or where they came from. What I know is she's still hell-bent on using Cataclysm and believe me, she'll bring fire down on us all."

I asked, "And what are the Omegans bringing?"

Zengus said, "Don't matter what they're bringing. They're coming to shut all of this down. We've lived on their graces for generations at the cost of giving them everything this planet has. What would you have expected?"

"I don't know, Zengus. Can't see what you could expect from them other than to be their dog," Kado said.

Zengus said, "Better a live dog than a dead duck. You're going into the mill. Least I'm making my plans to get away somehow. Now let's move."

With Zengus and Reilly watching, we formed a detail and hauled the Cataclysm device out of the cave. The box was more bulky than heavy, and I kept an eye on Zengus and Reilly, who both trained their guns on us.

I was next to Kado, and we stood across from Norg. Norg's eyes still had the glazed bluish glow to them, and he said nothing other than a few grunts when the box got stuck against a wall of the tunnel.

Our trip out of the cave was a lot bumpier and quieter than the way in, of course. Reilly walked ahead while Zengus watched us from the rear. I heard Zengus open up his comm. "Cataclysm retrieved transport. Give ETA."

The comm crackled for a few seconds; then came a response. "ETA ten minutes."

Zengus replied, "Good work. How about the others?"

After a few seconds the comm crackled again. "Crucinal and Firebreed? Lost contact with their transport but we saw the blast. No one walking away from that."

My knees weakened.

No, it couldn't have been.

She'd have fought back, right? Wouldn't she have figured out there was a problem? Ana was too smart for that, just to have been locked up and killed.

By the time we made it outside, the transport ships had landed. Their slender black crafts were lined up as if on a showroom floor somewhere. They'd been over our vehicle already, and from the mess of wiring and pieces thrown around, it was a safe bet we were stranded.

Some of the Lebabolis gray bands approached. Zengus motioned them to the Cataclysm device. While others grabbed Kado and me, Norg loaded the device onto one of the transports. They brought us close to our craft.

"On your knees," Zengus commanded.

"Zengus, what's the point now? You've got Cataclysm, Charista has it. Why even waste time on us when you can destroy whoever you want?" I asked.

Zengus said, "Because this was part of the deal. Charista doesn't want anyone around who could get in the way. Which is why she had Ana killed as well."

He watched us as the words sank in. I eyed Kado; he just watched Zengus with eyes so wide and his mouth halfway open. "You unbelievable bastards."

"That's enough from you two." Zengus swung his rifle to my chest. "I think I'll take away the prophet here, since he started all this."

My eyes were blurred with tears and I choked a few sobs out. Was this it for me? Was this how it was going to end? Dying alone here centuries in the future, and what did I have to show for it? Not a whole hell of a lot.

Zengus closed one eye and took aim, but Reilly stopped him. "We got trouble."

Zengus still held his aim. "Who, Omegans?"

"No, something else—you've got to see this." Reilly pointed at something over our shoulders.

Zengus flung his rifle across his back and leaned close. His stale breath had me gag a bit. "Stay right here; I'll be back to finish the job in a second."

I craned my neck for a look at whatever they saw, but the Hell

Hawk and the transports blocked my view. But then I heard a noise.

At first it sounded like rolls of thunder. As it got louder, it cleared up—it wasn't thunder but a lot of yelling. A group approached from hills off to the left of the cave across a clearing. None of them looked familiar, and they weren't even Omegans. In fact there were no distinguishing colors or anything. All of them had scraggly manes of hair. In the front of them was a man with a Hell Hawk pilot uniform. I chuckled when I noticed the mane of blonde hair on the man ahead of the group and the crazy look in his eyes.

"I'll be damned," Kado muttered.

"What?" I asked.

"It's Jacobs."

"How can you tell this far away?"

Kado chuckled. "I'd know that mop of hair anywhere."

There he was, his uniform more ragged from when I'd last seen him at the crater, but it was the guy, his eyes wild, but the group he was with I hadn't seen. I scanned the crowd for any hint of Ana, but she wasn't there.

Who were these new friends? Had he lost his mind and hooked up with renegade savages? Whoever they were I just hoped they were on our side. The other soldiers were pretty haggard, but their shoulders were broad and they carried weapons. Some were pulse rifles, some just sticks, but they looked menacing.

Zengus waved the Lebabolis detail, and they loaded up onto the ships. Before long, the night air erupted in pulse fire.

Jacob's group kept their charge up and just broke off into multiple units. They peppered the Transports with pulse fire in random short bursts. The Lebabolis troops hunkered down and laid down fire. The ground shook from the explosions and weapons blasts.

Zengus, rifle held up against his side, dashed back to us.

"On second thought, we may need some help with Cataclysm once it gets going." He clutched Kado by the scruff of his neck. Kado yelled out and fumbled until he was upright. Zengus dragged him off to the ship. I watched him pass Norg, and he swung his rifle into the side of Norg's head. Norg collapsed onto the ground.

Zengus and his group fired up their ships and after return fire from the group with Jacobs, they were up and soared out of sight in a few seconds.

The troops made it to the Hell Hawk, and when they saw me some of them growled in response. But Jacobs waved the others down. He walked close to me, the rest of them close behind. They'd have all been shoo-ins for extras on an episode of *The Walking Dead*.

"The hell are y'all doin here?" Jacobs lifted me to my feet.

"I was thinking the same thing about you," I responded.

He shrugged and laughed. "We got hit after the Crater. Omegan bastards shot my bird up good, had to ditch inside Lebabolis territory.

"You landed?" I asked.

"Hell, yeah, I did. Who the hell you think you're talkin' to?"

"What about Ana?"

"She's fine, least since we landed. We parted ways on our next move. Ana and Dawn took off with Treg for the Capital, rest of us wanted back in the fight."

I felt a lump form in my throat. "They said they killed her."

"Who?"

"Zengus."

"What happened to him?" Jacobs asked.

"Went traitor," I said. "Turned this guy into a drone, at least for a while." I motioned to Norg. He stood up straight, like a machine that waited for its next command.

Jacobs eyed Norg. "Ehh, yeah, well, some of these Guard been working around tech things. I'll have them take a look. Long as Norg ain't trying to take us down for now. So back up a bit. You said Zengus turned?"

"Yep. We'd gotten our hands on Cataclysm and he overpowered us. Took off on those craft you shot at with Kado."

Jacobs rubbed his eyes and took a deep breath. "I just don't know. If Charista gets that thing and can get it to work, I just…" He stared off in thought about what the rest of his comment would've meant, and I had an idea it was something pretty horrific on a global scale. He seemed to also be processing the fact that Cataclysm even existed, as if he'd been an agnostic suddenly shown how wrong they were about the beyond.

His eyes cleared a bit, and then they showed pain as he said, "Ana, gone?" His eyes got misty and he bowed his head for a second. "She was our link; she pulled us together."

His body softened a bit and I felt more tears come down. There had to be a mistake. Zengus just wanted us as broken and defeated as possible. I had to think this was just some mind game of his.

"Who are these people?"

"The Guard."

"Yeah?"

"You bet your ass. They been tearing it up in the Outlands. They're scattered but in groups large enough to cause some serious hell, I'm here to tell ya. We been giving Omegans plenty of crap to deal with."

"That's great but there's more. They struck a deal."

"What?"

"Something about a package exchange. Kado intercepted a transmission," I said.

Jacobs wiped his brow and cast a look around toward the Guard troops. "Package? What, the Valentium?"

I grabbed his arm. "No, you don't understand. The package isn't Valentium at all. It's us."

His face twisted a bit. "Come again?"

"That's right, Jacobs. The Coalition wasn't ever being sent to the Range to fight the Omegans. We're being delivered to them."

"By who?" Jacobs asked.

"Charista."

Jacobs shook his head and took a few uneasy steps around. He looked over the Guard troops. They looked pretty eager for some action, one way or the other.

Sweat glistened his already filthy brow. He swiped at his eyes a bit. "So they get their weapon and they get to turn us loose. For what, I haven't a clue. I- I told Ana she shouldn't have trusted Charista. I tried stopping her, Nelson. I did."

"I know. Tell you the truth, I don't believe that story about her being dead. Just seems too simple for them to try that. They'd do anything to shake us up," I said.

In an instant, Jacobs shook his head and reared up, as if he'd gotten some kind of electric shock. His eyes steeled a bit and his brow uncreased. "Hmm, well, we can't sit here thinking about what might be while there's something pretty big we can do something about."

"The Range," I said.

He nodded. "Something else too, and this lines up with what you said about us being delivered to the Omegans. We've been tracking a large group of Omegans, hitting them when we could, but they ain't stopping for shit, and my best guess on where they're headin' is smack dab where Llewyn is. If we've been sold out, I'm circling back and protecting who I care about that I'm sure's still here. Our people need us; I'm going there. Y'all coming?"

"Hell, yeah. So Llewyn made it to the Range?"

Jacobs nodded. "Yep, well, he best get tucked in quick because there's Omegan patrols all over the place. They're gonna hit the Range hard, and he better be locked in."

"How'd you get in with this group?"

"When I left Ana and the rest at the crash site, I headed for the nearest Storehouse I could think of. It took a while, but then I ran into these guys. It took some convincing but not too much to get them to realize I was no friend of Omegans and definitely not Lebabolis. They brought me to one of their encampments and showed me their setup."

"How many are there out there?"

"This group's five hundred strong right now, but they tell me there's over a thousand, spread around the Outlands. They live apart though; they forage for whatever they can find in the wild and the Outlands."

"Who's their leader?"

"Some guy named Duncan. He ain't interested in getting involved in any combat. They want to keep themselves fed."

"If they got word, if Llewyn called a distress alert, they'd already known about it."

"Maybe but we've got a package out there, Valentium."

"Yeah? That's his big plan? Don't add up at all, man. They're corralling us in. And now we're going to the Range, a dead end. They've got us penned in. What if it wasn't about the Valentium after all?"

"What are you saying?"

"This whole exchange is bullshit. The package they want to trade isn't the Valentium, it's a hostage exchange. They're trading us."

"But for what?"

"We need to get in the open on this. Let's circle around the Range. If the Omegans are gonna hit that, we need to be where they wouldn't expect us. That's what Ana'd want anyway."

Chapter 16 (Ana)

C HARISTA WALKED ME OVER to Harkson's private quarters where he met me. He was the biggest mystery to me of all the upper echelon of Lebabolis, even more than the Coursons. At least the Coursons were known in the Sectors, and every now and then they showed up in different places, but Harkson was out of sight most of the time. The updates on MODOSNet pretty much all featured Charista with the status of Lebabolis, and Harkson was a ghost in the wind who ran things from some distant place or even another planet.

He sat at his desk slouched as if a king who'd held his reign too long and had gotten fat and bored. His cold eyes examined me inside and out like he was some kind of judge who decreed a verdict on a crime he also determined I committed.

Everything was bathed in dark colors. A wall of monitors filled one side; each screen showed activity from a different Sector. Most of them had Omegan Patrols at one point or another. I couldn't believe how they were so comfortable with this; at least they never said anything about it to me. We were supposed to be in this pact together, but it was clear how much they withheld the longer I stayed over here.

The terminal at Harkson's desk was pushed to the side, and he clutched a glass. His steel grey eyes looked like they'd seen the world and then some. He looked tired but also like he'd just

172

read the book about my life and was ready to quiz me on it.

"I trust Charista told you about the Valkyrie?" He said the word 'Valkyrie' like it was a piece of sour fruit in his mouth or a bacterial infection. His brow drew in a line.

"She showed me the clips."

His eyes still locked on me, he sipped from his glass. "I never liked the Valkyrie. That much power in one person's hands is a recipe for disaster. But these aren't normal times, and people having a focal point drives them more than anything else. People are easy to sway if you've got their emotions. I can't deny the Valkyrie did that quite well. She convinced them freedom was better than security, in fact."

He reached back and tapped the terminal at his desk, and up sprung a holo image of the Valkyrie symbol. He shook his head at the crossed dagger and bolt as if it were an insect he wanted killed.

"Isn't that contraband here?"

Harkson studied the image a little more, then returned my glance with more of his icy gaze. "It was, during peacetime. Symbols are very powerful, Ms. Crucinal, as you may have realized by now. They rally people, give them something to fight for." His lips curved up just a little as he added, "Against unbeatable odds."

I pulled the knife and turned it over and around in my hands. "What does any of this have to do with me?"

His brow raised and he chuckled a little. He looked uneasy about having laughed. I figured there weren't many laughs around here, ever. "So she didn't tell you everything?"

I sighed and slapped the knife on his desk. His eyes jumped to it, then back to me. I leaned closer. "No. How about you do before I raid your supplies and leave with my brother?"

It felt like I was back with Baudricort. There wasn't a word for how done I was with all this mystery and secrets. "I want to know about—"

"Ana, the woman Petra you've seen... the Valkyrie... she's your mother."

I froze in place. My gut was burning, and I heard almost

nothing except the ringing in my ears. "What? No, m-my dad was taken as a Deviant and sent for Realignment and my mother was a Worker Product killed in a raid."

Harkson shook his head. "The people you lived with as your parents were in fact taken as part of the Deviant uprising, and yes they were sent for Realignment. We pieced together records in MODOSNet after Baudricort wiped all he did from the system and formed the Action. He covered a lot of tracks; I guess he was worried we'd target any offspring of Deviants and do away with them."

"Wonder how he got that idea."

He ignored my glare. "As I said earlier, the symbol of the Valkyrie was very important at one time. She saved Lebabolis from being overrun, and a lot of people remembered those days. But once it came time to reestablish order and preserve the peace, the Valkyrie was at odds with the plans of the Coursons."

"I've heard this story. She tried to take control back and ended up killing Products, then she disappeared once she went to face a group of Omegans who attacked Lebabolis."

"That's not all of it. The Valkyrie is a wartime leader and we were at peace, but she wouldn't stand down, and she had enough people on her side to be a problem. Ana, that's not all. She killed people. Among them, your mother. Instead of a discussion, she opted for a takeover. It threatened our security. We had to stop her for the safety of it all."

The video showed scenes of Sector Five, a fabrication plant. The one my mom worked at.

"Sector Five produced window tech. This is security footage from when the Valkyrie assaulted the complex. She called it liberation, but this; look, Ana. Look at those people. Terrified, running and being slaughtered."

I watched an army, led by the Valkyrie, proceed through the plants, firing on security and other soldiers. People were laid down in her wake. She regarded the scene with a smug smirk on her face.

He took a sip of his drink. "Ana, you know what's happening out there now. You're closer to it than anyone here. You've seen the bodies and destruction. Not even our best Radomet can hold off this invasion forever."

"Why didn't he just tell me? I was with him for so long, he had every opportunity to, but he never said anything about this." A tear stung my eye when I painfully recalled how slow he even was to reveal he was my father.

"Charista gave you who we want; I'm telling you what we need. We've had to make hard choices. Charista and I don't always agree, but on this we do. We are luring the Omegans into a trap. We've got it set up: fake vehicles, some Hell Hawks, and beacons to simulate enough of a Valentium deposit. They've been after the Valentium more and more; we'll give them their chance to take a huge haul in."

"What makes you think they'll bite? They've been pretty damned strategic so far, from what I've seen."

"It's a risk. We're coordinating with Jason and Kaitlinn. They'll begin maneuvers to draw the Omegans they're in contact with into a path for this location. Once you find Cataclysm, you activate it and hit the distress beacon."

I shuddered at this news. Baudricort had wanted no risk for me or the Action, so he kept that identity a secret. As recorded as it was in MODOSNet, he was able to change those records enough to not be a concern, then put me with the parents who raised me. I felt a lump in my throat at that thought. What did he or they do that they were so ready to take me on. I felt an ache for them, even if they weren't who had me naturally, they were still there for me while I grew up.

"Yeah, I'm out there fighting, and I'll keep on doing it, but what are you suggesting that's any different? Why me, anyway?"

"Who better to become the Valkyrie than her offspring?" The words hung in the air like the echo of a pulse cannon blast. I had no response at first. His eyes pleaded with me. He grasped my arm.

"You were born for this. Take lead of the forces. I know they've used you, but you've got competition. Jason and Kaitlinn are running a lot over there. Llewyn was a ranking member in Lebabolis; you think he'll stay with the Action and accept your freedom? He was with Baudricort, he wanted you dead. Who do you think it was who tried to have you killed? It was him! They are becoming egotistical. Leaders always have a danger of becoming too absorbed in their own glory and forgetting the true mission, the true purpose of why they're there. But you, Ana Crucinal. Not only are you the offspring of the true Valkyrie, you wanted only to save your brother and your fellow people in the Action.

"Some people already say I'm the Valkyrie."

"What do you say? Are you ready to stop listening to what other people think you should be and become what you are? Now is your chance. You thought nothing about running through a Verge centuries in the past because of what Baudricort wanted. You're who we need; who they need. When people see you leading the forces, it will turn the tide. It has to."

"And if it doesn't?"

He watched me for a few moments. He leaned back in his chair and folded his arms in thought. I looked back at the monitors that showed Omegan patrols in contact with a group led by Kaitlinn. The Omegans lit up the screen with fire, and the Action scampered about. The monitors were a collection of chaos. I wondered what else they had in mind if this plan failed. They were so outnumbered, so helpless. What would one person change about that?

"What about when it's over and you've got Cataclysm, and we're still apart from you? We won't join your fold again. We're living free or you might as well kill us, starting with me right now."

"Ana, we want peace, like you. We want things settled. I don't want to house these people forever like livestock. There's no point to keeping that going, as long as there is no more danger, and that's what I and the rest want, no more danger. You do too, right? That's the whole reason you left in the first place. I want things to return to how they were. We'll discuss terms when the time comes. You must understand though, this role you have ends when the war does. And once we give you what we've promised, our agreement terminates into peace unless you decide to challenge us again."

"You cross me, I'll blow Cataclysm sky high and take you all to hell with me."

"I think you're smart enough to know we have as much on the line as you do."

"Yeah, but I've also learned how trusting anyone, even someone who says they're an ally, can be dangerous."

I watched his face. He held my gaze and smiled. "You're wise, like your father."

My thoughts went to Kado, and how I bet even right then he tinkered somewhere on a solution that would change the outcome.

"You'll need to step up your arsenal," I muttered. "They've got disruptors. Any powered devices like guns and vehicles on the ground and in the air are disabled by 'em. It won't be long before they overrun us with that. And even with the Capital sectioned off, you know that won't keep them away from your front door for long."

The comm on Harkson's desk buzzed.

"Chancellor, urgent message from the Coalition. They've made the Range but are engaged with a large force of Omegans. Requesting assistance at once."

Harkson was silent. He pulled a P-LAD out and flipped it around in his hands for a minute or so. He gazed off, his eyes in a daze. Then he looked at me. "Ready to do your part of the deal?"

I shifted up in my seat. "What?"

"The Valkyrie led this nation before when the Omegans attacked, and that was how we kept ourselves safe from them. Now we need that to happen again. And though we don't have the Valkyrie, I think we've got the next best thing... Ana Crucinal, darling of the Action. The girl who outfought Radomets and risked her life to save her brother."

I heard him go on about these stories about me as if they were bedtime tales. It felt weird hearing this again, this time from the leader of Lebabolis himself. I shook my head. Harkson's forehead wrinkled. "I'm not sure you're thinking this all the way through, dear. Varrick was healed, part of the deal you and Charista sealed. We kept our end of the bargain—"

"The only thing we had to face back then was the attack on Sector Five." I gripped the arms of my chair tightly.

"Our deal was to turn back the Omegans."

"Why does it have to be me? Besides, some of my own people haven't taken to the idea of me in command."

Harkson chuckled and stood up. He walked about the desk. "Oh dear Ana, respect for the rank and respect for the person aren't the same. You've passed up a lot of people who are older and have been soldiers longer. How did you expect them to handle you as their leader?"

He grabbed a black rectangular shaped box and set it on the table. After he tapped a few controls the device opened and displayed several bracelets inside. "I can't mind control anyone, at least not anymore. The Link was damaged too much from all of the Valentium disruptions. However, people will remember these. We're spreading the word that the Valkyrie has returned, and it's you. And we're sending another unit to help protect your friends at the mountain range. We need you to be the Valkyrie though. To believe it for yourself. To know that you are the one, the person who will stop these attackers. The warrior who will restore peace."

I eyed the strange bracelets before me. The Valkyrie was always such a legend, I swore she was fifteen feet tall and crushed rocks with her bare hands. The thought of someone else being the Valkyrie was a little much to take.

I also doubted what effect it would have. Sure, the Valkyrie turned back the Omegan invasion in the early years, but from what I had heard that was much smaller than what they faced this time. And what exactly would that do that the Lebabolis military and other products couldn't also do?

"Ana, I need you. Lebabolis needs you. Your friends in the Action need you. We're sending a company of forces with a squadron of Transports. You'll be travelling much faster, so their Darkness shouldn't be a problem. You'll sweep down on the Western Range and catch the Omegans. They'll be off guard. Once you hit, the Action and Lebabolis troops in the field will engage from the sides and catch them off guard. They'll be caught by surprise, and if the weaponry the Action is developing is ready, you'll be able to turn them back."

I gripped the blade in my hands and ran my fingers over the sigil. The crossed blade and lightning bolt that represented freedom. At least, freedom for Lebabolis. I wondered if they included anyone else in that number. They had given Varrick his life back, and the rest of the sick from the Pox, so there was that.

The troops I saw here were pretty big in number. I wasn't sure how many were left for defense, but if I knew anything about Charista, she'd never leave her back door unguarded. She was way too careful about that.

I felt a mixture of good and uneasy about Harkson's suggestion I take the lead here. What was it about me that Llewyn and even Kaitlinn never took seriously when I led that group with the Coalition? Was I just the dumb young girl, even now? The one who never listened, who went off on her own, who dared jump through the Verge even though she was never prepared for it? I wished I knew how to wait at times, how to hold my tongue, to keep silent and let others speak. But silence to me was the worst pain of all. Of all the things I'd become tired of, the worst was having to wonder what people wanted me to be. It was time I drew my own line in the sand and let everyone know about it.

"I do this—" I clutched the blade and eyed Harkson—"we establish our new home in the Western Range, and you show us the shield technology so we set it up for ourselves."

Harkson clasped his hands. His lips protruded and he narrowed his eyes at me. Then, his face softened and he laughed a bit. "See, negotiating your terms. I knew you were a leader. Yes, of course. Contact me when this is over, and we'll set up terms for bringing our shield capability to yours."

I watched the blade on the dagger. The Voice said nothing, and for once it hadn't bothered me. This was my call, just like the others had been, and I knew I had to stick by this. Baudricort wasn't there for help. Neither was Llewyn or Kaitlinn or anyone else in power. It was me, the one they'd chosen. It was my time.

My back was still protected anyway, as long as I had one of my Circle with me. If I had Treg and got near Norg or Zengus, I had a chance. Worst case, I'd lead these troops into the battle and let them duke it out with the Omegans.

I felt a surge burst through me, not because of who Harkson and Charista were, but because of who I was. "OK." I stood up, my hand extended. "It's a deal. Show me to the troops and let's get started."

Chapter 17 (Ana)

O UR GROUP OF SEVEN transports left Lebabolis after sunset and soared on a direct course for the Western Range, I hoped in time to make a difference and keep the Action safe. I rode with Treg in the lead ship, because in spite of what they showed and told me, I just knew I was never all the way safe unless I had one of the Circle close by. The deal was tricky, having Treg on board was not.

The Transport shook and yawed about a little as it rocketed to supersonic speed. We'd come in pretty fast when we got there, but that may have been all it took to catch the Omegans off guard. I braced my hands against the walls, but in a few minutes, I realized that wasn't necessary. This ship hadn't vibrated like a Hell Hawk, even as fast as we went. The angry howls of the engines were gone too. Instead, a steady hum was the only thing that let me know we weren't still on the ground.

I wondered about Harkson's reasons for this sudden burst of support. They wanted the Omegans gone, fine. But they had already given us an army. The Action had gear, even at the Range. Harkson stretched Lebabolis protection out a bit thin with these moves; I hadn't figured out his logic on that yet.

I watched the troops at the pilot console. They weren't mine anymore than I was theirs. I looked for some spark or fire in their eyes, but all I saw was a dull coldness. They were under orders from Harkson, not me, and it made me nervous that we may just have to depend on them if shit got serious.

I sat in the rear of the cockpit and watched the pilots as they monitored and adjusted controls without a word. The only response I really got from them was a salute.

Treg waited in the lower hold with the ground troops, in case one of 'em had anything in mind like our little exploding pod from earlier.

One of the pilots spoke, and I just about slipped out of my seat from the surprise at the sound of their voice. "ETA to Western Range, thirty minutes."

His comm buzzed with a reply from the lower hold. "Roger that, ground units on standby."

One pilot glanced my way. One of his eyes was covered with a red lens from the ship navigation tool. "We'll drop ground troops off on a ridge about a click from the Range. That's enough space for them to set up and start their Landcrawlers up. We'll support them from the air after that."

"What kinda guns you got on this bird?"

"Oh, they aren't loaded like Hell Hawks, but they've got pulse cannon. Enough for moderate damage."

I nodded. "OK. So, you got a name or should I call you 'hey you'?"

His face stayed fixed on me, but there was no hint of a smile. He just replied, "Jarin."

"Thanks, Jarin." I leaned forward toward him. "Harkson or Charista tell you about me?"

He shrugged. "Just that you're leading this attack and to take orders from you. I don't know much more than that. I'm told what I need and I guess that's it for now."

"Right." My mind's eye laid out the scene of the fight, as much as I'd known about it. I closed my eyes and took a slow breath. "Once we let the ground troops go we should pull back until they get in position so we can hit the Omegans at the same time as the Landcrawlers, give them more support."

Jarin nodded a little and looked back my way again. "Roger that. We begin deploy procedures in fifteen, better get into seat restraints."

The roar and rumble of the engines built to a loud ear-splitting noise. Our craft dipped down and I saw the others alongside us doing the same, releasing the Landcrawlers and troops so they could get in position.

Jarin studied a few digi maps on his console. An alert beep sounded with a message on the console, but Jarin covered it pretty quick. Not quick enough that I hadn't seen it, though.

I ducked back outside the cockpit to the access way to the below compartments and met up with Treg. Back when we were kids and he was just a Warrior Product trainee and illegally shared information with me, he had told me how it was always important to talk in code if I was ever in a hostage type situation.

"Hey, you OK back here?"

"Mmmhm. They're loading up gear. Should be another two, three minutes before we're out. How are you?"

"I saw some really strange trees at the Capital, forgot to mention it to you. Did you notice?"

Treg paused, and responded slowly. "Like what?"

"It was just these roots. They were really twisted."

"Oh yeah, that's bad. How'd they look up top?"

"Not good. Someone needed to cut 'em down."

Treg paused for a while, then he replied, his voice slow and steady. "Check." His eyes steeled, and he took a few deep breaths.

By the time I made it back to the cockpit, the stars greeted me like a twinkling cloth that covered the outer glass of the ship.

Jarin commented, "A few more minutes, we can swoop in and hit them all at once."

The comm chatter was filled with the other craft giving statuses, weapons checks, everything. If this punch was everything we needed, Kaitlinn's crew should be able to bust in and finish these guys off.

I grabbed my rifle and checked it over. A strange beeping noise came from somewhere. I flipped the rifle around and looked near the power supply. Nothing. I activated the firing mechanism for a test; it looked fine. My comm wasn't being activated either.

What was that noise?

I glanced up and saw something on the console for a second, but Jarin's hand swept over it.

It was an auto destruct sequence.

I kept looking at my rifle and then I held it across my lap.

"Everything OK, Jarin?"

He kept working on the console. "Of course, why?"

My hand grasped the handle of my gun tight. I felt the blood rush to my face.

"I was just wondering why you activated the self-destruct. Something you wanna share with me?"

An electrical zap hit my right shoulder. A thousand tingling daggers stabbed into me, and my arm flung out, sending the rifle tumbling loudly to the floor. Jarin's co-pilot had electro tased me.

"What are you—"

"Shut up!" Jarin left his seat and stood before me. "This is our mission, and I'm afraid it doesn't involve you or your Action."

He grabbed my right arm, still limp from the blast, and placed a restraint on it. I struggled a bit with the left until he shoved me down and jammed his knee into my left shoulder.

"Is that right?" I groaned as he fastened both my hands together and hoisted me back into a seat.

"Completely. You see, other negotiations were made. And Harkson felt it was best he put all his bad eggs in one basket. So we'll turn our troops back to where they'll do some real good, and you and your Action friends can deal with the Omegan horde. I'm sure they'll have a good time turning you into dust."

Jarin and his co-pilot set a few more controls on the console before they turned to leave the cabin, with me still tied down. Jarin paused and clutched my shoulder. He shook his head, a look of pity on his face. "I expected more from a Valkyrie."

I tugged hard against my bindings. My hands ached to go for his throat, but it was no use. The craft wobbled a bit and started to dip downward. Jarin and his co-pilot braced themselves. When they opened the door to the cabin, I heard that battle tested and weary voice who'd never let me down since we were young.

"Yeah, no, this really won't work, you tying my friend up. Your mama didn't raise you better than that?"

I craned my head back to the sight of Treg as he swung at the co-pilot. Jarin ducked aside and grabbed the electro tase again. I writhed in my seat until I flopped to the floor. I crouched as best I could then launched myself toward Jarin. It was all I could do, but if anything I'd take another jolt and give Treg a chance to do away with these guys.

Unfortunately, the co-pilot got his own stun weapon out and knocked Treg downward. Jarin swiped a fist at me and I plummeted back down to the floor. Jarin and the other crew bolted down the hallway.

"You OK?" I yelled. I tried to sit upright but the wobbling ship made it almost impossible.

"Yeah, great," Treg muttered. "So Harkson gave us the raw deal?"

"Whatever gave you that idea? He and Charista are in on this cluster, and I owe them both a world of shit. How bad they zap you?"

"Oh, my ass has felt better."

"Thanks for the update."

"Anytime."

We could both hear the beeping from the console.

"You've got to be kidding me," Treg said, clambering toward the controls.

"No joke. They set the auto destruct and if we can't stop that, we gotta bail."

"What about the crew?"

"Sensor panel indicates they sprung the emergency troop release."

Treg jumped into the pilot seat. I made my way closer to see the console over his left arm. The readout showed the destruct sequence activated with a minute to spare.

"I don't know this ship. It's new tech."

"You gotta do something, Treg." Treg groaned as he tugged the control stick back and forth. The craft slowly pulled back out of its dive.

"OK, so we won't smash into the ground." Treg eyed the console. "They changed these up. The Hell Hawks had an energy discharge relay by the pilot seat. If we can find and yank it that should disable the onboard system. At least it worked like that in the Hell Hawks."

"Give me the downside."

"I'll have to land this metal manually."

"You can swing that?"

"I can drop this bucket. It won't feel too good, but I can handle what she's got," Treg said. He thrust his hands downward. I strained against my restraints. My wrists burned as the couplings around them dug into my flesh.

The timer got to forty seconds. Treg fished his hand about wildly, then he paused, his eyes widened and a smile formed. "That's gotta be it."

Treg moved the handle and the console buzzed with a warning. "Energy discharge selected. Enter code to confirm." A set of number keys appeared.

"Oh, great," I groaned.

"We gotta bail." Treg flung me into the co-pilot seat and attached the restraints as much as he could with my arms still bound. He jumped into the seat and activated the pilot eject sequence. In seconds we rocketed out of the craft straight up into the air.

The canopy flipped away and fell back to the ground. I watched the Hell Hawk career back toward the ground, and a few seconds later it exploded and sent a blast of hot air and smoke in our direction.

Parachutes on our seats deployed, and we slowly dropped to the ground. I saw the other transports in the distance, along with a few groups of ground troops headed toward the Range.

Treg and I landed fifty yards apart. Once he freed himself he came over and helped unfasten my wrists.

"Shoulda known she'd set us up." I shook my head. "All that talk about coordinates and finding Cataclysm. Guess she figured on another deal. Why did I do this again?"

"Nelson." Treg looked at me.

"If Dawn did a Link pull on me, she'd have gotten the coordinates. But she couldn't have done that while I was asleep." My thoughts drifted to that research lab I was ushered away from by Harkson. "They must've found another way to it. Nelson's useless to them now. He's not in their system or subject to a Pull. Baudricort was lucky he got what he did out of him."

"Once again, Charista missed her target." I clutched my wrists. "Don't suppose you got any weapons outta there before we ditched."

Treg frowned. "Coulda kicked myself, not grabbing one of those morons' rifles on the bridge. Well, sit tight. We just—"

Treg was looking past my shoulder, and his eyes widened. If he was shocked by something, then I knew we were in trouble. I quickly turned around to face our next obstacle.

There was a large group of Lebabolis soldiers approaching us.

Thankfully, their weapons were down. I recognized an officer insignia on one of them in the front. I saw his tag read the name "Clyde". He waved the rest to a halt and came close to us.

"You're Ana, the Valkyrie?"

I smirked a bit. "Some people think so."

Clyde nodded. His face was strewn with sweat and a bit of brownish oily liquid. I pointed toward his face. "You been through a rough ride, huh?"

He wiped a hand at the liquid on his face and checked it. "Yeah, well, Charista never told us one objective of this mission was taking you out."

I clenched my gut. Treg frowned and gave a small chuckle as he shook his head.

"Is that right?" I narrowed my eyes. "What's your wait, then? I'm here, aren't I? Unarmed?"

Clyde watched me. His eyes weren't cold, though. They looked more like that of a fatigued animal. "Don't make sense to. I been fighting and killing people who never fell in line. Deviants couldn't make their lives fit any kind of mold Lebabolis said they should. And now Omegans are destroying all we got and making it disappear. Making us a thing of the past, too. Well, I got to thinking how much Lebabolis took away, much more than they ever gave. It's time I fight for someone who's gonna work for me, not just work me. We have to work together, or we don't work. One or None."

"Yeah? What about your crew there?"

Clyde motioned to the rest near him. "We're all in the same unit. Warrior Products from Lebabolis. Never joined the Action, but that doesn't mean we liked everything they had us do. And now, with the Omegans... we're not fighting against each other anymore. There's too much at stake. We're with you... the Valkyrie."

I looked at Treg. "I'm not sure I'm the one you think I am. But if you wanna help me, our friends are in trouble. We're heading over the next few ridges ahead; that should bring us close to the fight. There's a lot of Omegans trying to get into the Ridge. I have no idea what the others from Lebabolis are gonna do since Jarin and several others tried to have us killed back there."

"We've got weapons. Don't have a Landcrawler; ours was disabled," Clyde said.

"That never stopped the Valkyrie before, did it?" I looked at 'em and suddenly felt very small. I'd held myself up for a while now. Being strong for Varrick, being tough for Treg. But now we were in this fight with people who'd faced down and defeated the Omegans years ago. Was I tough enough to fight alongside them?

Clyde said, "I'm not turning back from this. We need a plan."

I said, "Charista knows where Cataclysm is."

"Cataclysm? What do you mean?" Clyde asked.

"The device."

Clyde shook his head. "The Valkyrie was supposed to destroy it, but she was overrun. So she put in a security measure. Cataclysm cannot be operated without the security measure enacted."

"What measure?" I asked.

"It was on one of her last transmissions," Clyde said.

I thought back to Otto's P-LAD. "I have data from the Valkyrie, but I don't know the code." I showed the device to the others, but they stared at it with blank eyes. "I'm afraid we can't help you there. But we pledge ourselves and our young to you, the Valkyrie."

"Who are you, and how do you know all of this?" I asked.

Clyde opened the gap in his shirt and showed the mark of the Valkyrie in a brand on his chest. The crossed sword and lightning bolt had been covered by a layer of jagged and whitened hair from over the years, but the mark looked as if it was applied that day. A few of the others followed Clyde's gesture.

"You were with the Guard?" I asked.

Clyde smiled but shook his head. "We supported them and what they stood for. You too."

"Me? What do you mean?"

Clyde chuckled. "Oh, it was years ago, and you were pretty young. But we knew about you, and your parents."

My throat hitched.

"M-My parents?"

"The ones who raised you. They were good people." Clyde approached me and slid his arm around me. "They didn't deserve what happened to them, but they loved you as if you were their own."

I blinked tears from my eyes. The holes in my life hadn't hurt as much as long as I'd filled them with other things, but when I stopped and remembered things I'd never had, they pulled at me painfully.

I coughed so my sobs were stifled. "I know you're on the level now. I need you, and what's left of the Action needs you. The Omegans are after my friends, and neither of them realize where Cataclysm lies. But we have to watch Charista. She's on the prowl and will stop at nothing until she's got total control."

The soldiers formed a circle. They were disciplined and quiet. Their eyes had flickered with intensity, not the dull blankness that a lot of Products had in Lebabolis. Their arms were well toned, and they looked like an army without an arsenal.

They held their arms up in salute to me.

Suddenly I didn't see a hundred rough troops. I saw a thousand legions of deadly Guard members who I commanded. I felt like the greatest general in the world.

Chapter 18 (Nelson)

A FTER A QUICK REPAIR JOB, the craft we had was repaired enough to fly. I turned down a seat though. I'd had way more flying than I wanted for my lifetime. If I ever made it back I was starting a new personal rule: no trips that involve an airport.

Our group loaded up and trekked out toward the Range. After an hour's walk we heard the sounds of a fight. Pulse discharges, the periodic boom from an explosion. We topped a large hill and saw the scene.

There at the Range, the Action was holed up while the Omegans fanned out in an arc that cut them off. Smoke drifted all over the place, and the Omegans moved closer as they pummeled everything in their way.

Jacobs called the group over. "Listen up, that's our people over there taking fire. The ones you swore to protect once. I ain't talkin about Charista's lot. I mean those who were slaves and worked to death for nothing. You wanna get back at Charista, it starts with freein' those people. Remember, One or None!"

"One or None!" the crowd cheered.

The Guard troops formed a solid block formation. At the front they angled the lines and then gave the order to move out. I walked with Jacobs. Norg was nearby too. The blue glow had faded from his eyes, but they showed me nothing. He had to really be bad off to not have complained all this time.

After fifty feet, some of the Omegans noticed us and trained their weapons our way.

"Charge!" Jacobs yelled. The group lurched forward into a fast run, while the Hell Hawk soared above and angled several shots at the Omegans.

The ground rumbled with each blast from the Omegan ships. The Coalition forces returned fire as best they could and shot from every conceivable angle.

Another blast hit close and sent dust raining into my eyes. "We've got to get word to Llewyn! If we link up, we'll have a better chance of surviving this!" I yelled.

"Don't think we got time for that."

I squeezed the handle of my rifle. I'd just learned to shoot this damn thing, and now I was going to be killed. After all I'd been through. I guessed I'd never see dad again and now Ana was gone too. She died for this cause because these people were worth it. That meant to me this was right where I was supposed to be. I looked at Jacobs and Norg and couldn't have been prouder of who I was with.

In spite of how things were right then, a weird calm settled over me. I had a place, a point of existence. I even had a mission. I had to carry this out. My feet planted firmly into the ground.

A heavy rumbling built to our left and we saw Kaitlinn's troops appear from over a rise in that direction. The Hell Hawks glided over the soldiers and traded fire with the Omegans around the Range. Kaitlinn rode in a Landcrawler; she sat up top and directed the troops as they moved.

"She better watch, somebody gonna pop her out in the open like that," Jacobs muttered.

Jacobs Guard troops pressed forward into a melee with the closest Omegan division. They responded with a heavy barrage of pulse weapon fire. The darts of yellow hot light skewered the crowd, and screams came from all over when soldiers were hit. The group didn't slow down.

Norg stood next to me, silently. He looked to be coming out of that trance, but not all the way yet. I grabbed his arm. It was loud but I had to try.

"You in there, Norg?"

He surveyed the scene around us before his eyes slid to me.

"Norg, you alright?"

He had nothing in response. The best person who could've known what to do here was Kado, and he was long gone, maybe even dead. I thought about Ana again. The realization that I'd lost her, this woman, this character I'd somehow willed into existence. It felt more like I'd lost someone close. A friend or perhaps someone even closer.

I grabbed for a pulse rifle and fired shots back into the Omegan group. They had their own ships come down, and they peppered the area with another shower of fire. From this point, we had a chance to hook up with Kaitlinn's regiment but that meant we had to fight our way through a pretty thick line of Omegans that separated us.

The Action group drove the mobile facilities out into the crowd. They made it fifty yards before they were stopped with fire and turned into flaming roadblocks. The Action soldiers there fanned out on the sides of the flames and fired on the Omegans closest to them.

Jacobs bellowed, "We have to link up with Kaitlinn or Llewyn for any chance of making it out of this!"

I scanned around for the best way and asked Jacobs when I felt some taps on my midsection. I turned to Norg; his eyes were wide, and they gazed over my shoulder the other way.

Jacobs spoke before I turned around. "Son of a bitch."

"What?"

"Ms. Crucinal returns."

There she was.

I'd never seen anything like it—or her.

She was ahead of another group that looked a lot like the one with Jacobs. Some had Coalition uniforms, others looked more like another guard unit. Ana's face was twisted in a shriek, and they were at a full charge.

I watched the group and her and beamed with pride at her ferocity. I forgot where I was for a second. "Look at her. She's something else alright."

Jacobs nudged me. "Easy there, you sweet on her or something?"

I couldn't stop smiling, which made him laugh at me. It was strange to feel so happy in the middle of this fight, but at the same time, it was comforting.

Ana's group headed straight for the line of Omegans that divided us from Kaitlinn. Jacobs and I looked at each other, and he yelled out his command, "Pivot! Up the center!"

The Omegans who had been around earlier with the Valentium returned, and soon we were surrounded. The Omegans and their black and dark grey uniforms and ships closed in on us like an eclipse. With all of us there, there were at least three times as many of them.

The large device I'd seen at the center of them was lifted up in the air, and a low hum rattled and shook the ground. The pulse rifles around me made a weak fading beep sound.

"It's Darkness! They've activated it!"

The Coalition troops banged on and fumbled with their weapons for a few seconds, but it was useless. The Guard troops just flipped their guns around as if they were clubs and charged again. The Coalition troops followed along, and we continued our charge. The Omegans now unleashed more shots into our group, and more yelps and screams came from us in response.

The circle of Omegans around us got closer, but it made our group fight that much harder. This was our chance, and I had hope that Charista had another option, like Jason's regiment for assistance.

Whatever it was, time was running out, and we needed something fast.

Chapter 19 (Ana)

I HEARD THE ROAR of the Guard troops behind me, and they surged with more intensity than I'd ever seen, even more than the attack they made back in Sector Two. We charged right into the center of the Omegan horde, a mess of swung arms and deactivated pulse rifles. Their Darkness only stopped the weapons, not the highly pissed off people who swung 'em.

Out the corner of my eye, I noticed another group apart from the Omegans. They looked like the Guard, and before long I caught some Coalition garb in the mix. After several minutes, we made our way closer to this other group. I thought they were another unit ditched by Charista. But then Treg called out into the crowd.

"Norg! Nelson!"

I strained my eyes and ran toward them. Nelson was hunched over, and I saw his blood covered hand that grabbed his midsection. "What the hell happened to you?"

"Plenty. Let's start with Zengus."

"What?"

"He turned, Ana. He turned on us and took off with Cataclysm and Kado fifteen minutes ago."

The idea of my Circle being shattered again made me stand still. First Otto's death, now Zengus turning on us. Why?

Nelson yanked his rifle up and battered an Omegan who ran toward us in the head until it fell to the ground. Without missing a beat, he looked over at me and said, "He made a deal with Charista."

I stared at Nelson in disbelief. "Had a little training, have you?"

"I couldn't wait around for my bodyguard, now, could I?"

I bit my lip to stop myself from laughing. We were in the middle of a battle without any working weapons. Nelson held up his useless rifle.

"What are we going to do now?"

"The only thing we can. Fight. Don't leave my sight."

"Never again."

The air was filled with fire, energy sparks. This felt unusual; for once we weren't on the run from anyone. We ran toward and were in control.

"One or None! Attack and destroy 'em!" I shouted. My cries took on the sound of an angry predator. My pulse throbbed in my throat. I blinked back the red haze over my vision, but I soon realized it was my adrenaline in overdrive. My face flushed with heat. Suddenly these troops, these whatever they were, represented everything that stood in my way, and not just at this moment or this position. They were also the Lebabolis government that took my parents away. Charista, who dangled my brother and Nelson as her guarantee I'd be on the hook for whatever plan or objective she cooked up. And my mind had one thought in response. "Destroy them all!"

I felt rage course through my veins. My skin bristled, and my ears were filled with the roar of the fight. It made sense to me now, why this felt so right and normal.

I was bred for this.

Like my mother.

These enemies weren't Omegans to me anymore. A feeling took over me like an infection. Memories of seeing Varrick dying on an Action medical bed and how they hid him from me. The anger swelled so much that I hadn't felt the shot that pierced my side. Another fist glanced off my face. When I was close enough, I swung the butt of my rifle into the nearest Omegan. I took a hit to my midsection and doubled over for a second, but jumped back up and was in the middle of a giant fray that spread around me.

I saw their eyes, their inhuman eyes, images of hell and the dogs of Satan about them. They weren't human, and it made the blows that much easier to dish out. I felt the anger and rage as much a part of me as my own blood as what stood in my way, what kept me from the life I wanted, from the safety and security I needed for myself and my brother.

Llewyn came out and stood on top of one of the damaged facilities in the crowd that hadn't burned yet. He watched, and I yelled out to him to take cover, but it was no use. He wasn't concerned about taking a shot. A blind soldier with a rock could've taken him out. What the hell was he doing? Had he lost his mind?

The ships fired a little on us then moved back toward the group that came out of the cave. I saw Norg first; he took shots standing in the crowd. A few Omegans crumbled to the ground in agony when they were hit. Treg and I stood with our backs together and parlayed whoever came within range. I swung my arms until I felt like they couldn't move anymore, then I lunged into a large Omegan and drove them to the ground.

A hot stinging seared my right shoulder, and I saw a bloody blade being pulled out of me by a grinning Omegan. I connected with my good hand and knocked it to the ground. A deep soreness burst through my body. It got hard to breathe; even standing up straight was tough.

The howling around me was intense and kept going for what seemed like hours.

"Ana!"

I heard Nelson's voice but didn't see him. Then, there he was, among a group of soldiers with Norg. They fought their way closer, and we stood near each other, flailing arms, weapons, whatever we could grasp at the horde of Omegans. It felt like we were underground, the way they swarmed about us. Sweat rolled off my forehead and got into my eyes, making them sting.

197

"You alright?" he bellowed over the roar.

"Think so. Here we go again, huh?"

"Y-yeah, well. Same story, different day."

An Omegan swung a large pole over toward Nelson's head, and I swung my arm up fast to block it. The rod made a loud clang against my armor and glanced off. A tingling shot up my arm until my teeth vibrated. Nelson ducked at the sight of the weapon swung toward him, then looked up at me in amazement. A smile found his face. I felt removed from the fight, like I wasn't there at that moment anymore, that I was somewhere else with Nelson and this wasn't even a thought for us.

His eyes widened and brought me back in an instant. He reached his hand toward me, but then his eyes froze on something behind me. He shouted, but I didn't understand his words.

A searing sensation penetrated my lower back. The stinging scorch was soon replaced by a deep soreness. My arms and legs tingled and went limp. I wobbled on my feet, and there was a strange salty taste on my lips. I brushed a finger over my mouth and drew it back, coated with blood. Nelson shielded me as best he could with his own body.

Dizziness came over me as I shuffled around to a rather large Omegan. He had an insignia like Commander Chun, who we'd seen at Sector Five. I managed a shriek and raised my rifle, but he swung his fist into the side of my head. My feet slipped from under me, and I landed face down. Nelson was by my side, but his shouting soon faded. Everything around me, the screaming and explosions, paled to nothing. All around me was calm.

Then, I entered my own Darkness.

Chapter 20 (Nelson)

MY HEART FELL when I saw Ana's body go limp. The Omegan who'd shoved a spear into her back stood by and studied her body as it twitched at random.

"Ana!"

I swung my rifle at the Omegan who'd impaled her. The Guard who was nearby leapt around the Omegan and in a swift move snapped its neck.

The fighting continued as I sunk down near Ana and shielded her body from the combat above. The tears streamed down my face, and fear gripped me. What was going on, what were we supposed to do?

Pandemonium enveloped us like a dense fog. The Omegans continued their fight and we stood our ground best we could, but soon we were enclosed in a tight circle by the Omegan horde. I suddenly found myself pulled from the fight, and away from Ana, as much as I'd fought to stay close. I was then back in the scuffle on my feet.

A large horn sounded, and the Omegans stopped their assault. Our group pressed forward but all the Omegans did was defend at that point. Gradually, our group was subdued and the Omegans wrestled the few who still had strength to the ground. I then noticed I was near Llewyn. He regarded the scene with a grim frown, a trickle of blood oozing from a spot on his head.

"What's the plan?" I asked Llewyn.

He watched me with empty eyes, like his entire country had been destroyed. "Plan? We're a bit beyond that now." His eyes twitched about. The groans of the wounded settled on the battlefield. A group of Omegans on a small floating skiff observed the scene. One of them clasped a device and then spoke to us.

"Pitiful humans, you've lasted much longer than we'd ever expected. You've proven yourselves worthy of lasting for the purposes you've been designed for. My name is Emperor Zakmar of the Omegan empire, and you are henceforth and forever onward our prisoners. You were given the opportunity to serve us, but instead you defied our wishes. All you are, all that you did, all that you made was because we allowed you life. You won't win, you won't live, you won't breathe without us there. You're our crop, and we're reclaiming what is ours. We're taking you to our fortress soon. For now, do listen to what I say carefully and relinquish your weapons to the nearest Omegan at your side. Failure to do so will guarantee your immediate and swift termination. Do not test me; I've been gracious enough allowing you to come to this location freely."

The Coalition surrendered weapons slowly. The Omegans made their way through our group, pulling and reaching for our weapons. The wounded were sorted out. The dead were yanked out of the group, much to the anger of others nearby, but any attempts to stop the removal of bodies was met with brute force from the Omegans.

Before long a pile had developed of bodies. It pained me to look at it, but still I found myself focused on it. One of them reached for Ana.

"You're not taking her."

The soldier glared back at me and raised his hand to strike, but Llewyn grasped his shoulder and spoke a few words in his ear. He nodded and left Ana.

I shrugged and looked at Llewyn. "We've been down before; we can figure this out. I'm sure Charista's got a plan. Another strike, or Cataclysm maybe?"

Llewyn eyed me with a smirk, his eyes narrowed.

"She'd help us, right?"

Still with his eyes on me, he raised his hand. "Emperor Zakmar, I wish to discuss the terms of my surrender with you."

"Yes, we must discuss the terms of delivery as agreed upon by Charista."

I froze at the conversation.

It was him.

The whole time.

The familiarity that Llewyn had, the fact they knew him by name. Well, they'd know him by name because he was a ranking official. But the deal, the very terms that were mentioned in the document Kado uncovered. It wasn't fabricated, it wasn't a mistake. In fact, Llewyn looked to at least be in on it, maybe even the broker of the whole thing.

Llewyn eyed me with pity; a smile found his lips.

I felt rage as it coursed through me. My fists were balled so tight they got sore. "You unbelievable bastard. You sold us out to them. Why, what for? How the hell could you do this?"

"I'm here to survive, Nelson. Look around you. We've fought these people for decades. And you don't even realize we owe them for our very existence."

"What are you talking about?"

"Humans were dormant as a species. After countless wars humans had their biological activity suspended, and it was the Omegans who brought us back to life. They cloned, cultivated and trained us. They gave us some of their tech, which we learned and were even able to augment, like Cataclysm. We were supposed to be their workers, but something happened. While the Omegans were only worried about what they could take from the planet itself, we became aware and developed. Evolution took over and then before long we'd established a nation. With a whole belief system. And they had a harder time controlling us. People like the Valkyrie made it very difficult for us until they were taken by force to get us under control."

"What do you mean, 'us'? Wait, Llewyn—" I reached for

him.

He gazed on me with disgust. "Forget it, Nelson. That's how it is here, and if we don't make friends with it, we'll die. Charista is dealing, and I'm doing what I need to survive. I suggest you do the same."

"Dealing? With the same force who wants to kill us?"

"Corral, not kill."

I jabbed a finger toward Ana. "See what you did to her?"

He eyed Ana like someone who observed an entry at a science fair. All he mustered was a head shake. I lunged toward him, but an Omegan clutched me and flung me back to the ground.

I watched Llewyn's dead eyes review everything as he walked off. The whole place and everyone there looked frozen, like a streaming video caught in buffering mode. I felt numb and lost. The weight of this crushed me to where even breaths were difficult. This was my fault.

She couldn't be gone.

No.

Not her.

Not her too.

I couldn't lose her again. She lay there like a discarded mannequin, and I thought back to Mom's helpless and lifeless body on the bed. I clutched her while the rest were pulled and pushed into groups above and around me. I didn't care. It stung like Mom did. I lost her. Who was I, did it matter anymore? I wish it was me, why not me? It's my fault; why can't I just die so other people won't have to anymore?

I stared at Ana and noticed her brow wasn't creased. It was the first time I'd ever seen it relaxed, which made me all the more worried. Her eyes were shut. She lay like a wax figure. The Omegans prodded about the rest of us and divided people into groups. Large orcish looking soldiers stepped about with weapons, moving us into place like frightened cattle. A few who dared push back or resist were bludgeoned intensely.

One of the monitor screens across from us showed teams of Omegans hauling the Valentium store away. Just one of their precious cargoes. From the look of it they were far more gentle with it than with their human payload.

Some of the officers milled about. Zakmar stood fixed, his eyes pouring over us like a bear that is deciding which of us morsels were to be its next meal. "Your government has seen fit to deliver you to us in exchange for a cease fire. I'm not willing to discuss terms of this, and frankly, I could care less about their safety at the moment. We'll handle them in good time. But for now, all you need to know is you'll be transported for processing."

Zakmar strode about us. When he neared me I asked him, "What are we going to be doing there?"

Zakmar responded, "You'll find out soon enough. It's time you humans learn just how much you have was given to you, and since you've proven you can't be productive with your freedom, you'll be returned to the original purpose we developed you for: servants and miners. That is, those who can follow along. The rest, well, we've got ways of handling the non-compliant."

The leader of the Omegans spoke with Charista on a monitor chat, and in the background behind Charista I saw a large box being moved away with that familiar Valkyrie symbol on it. She had won, and the Omegans had no idea. To them, they'd made a deal and an easy grab. I wondered what they had in store for us.

Slavery?

Experimentation?

Worse?

None of it mattered anyway if Charista learned how to break the Cataclysm Failsafe. She had it, us and the Omegans where she wanted us. I thought back to a time that felt so long ago, when I was just a simple man who dreamed of writing this book. I had a crazy pie in the sky dream that I would get published one day, and now it had turned into this.

I held Ana's head on my lap. She was still as a rock, but I refused to believe she was gone. My mind flashed back to Mom on the bed, and my every thought that echoed the words and the sentiment, "Live, you must live! Don't do this."

I knew Mom had to go. But Ana; no, this was wrong. It was

too early and just incorrect.

"Don't leave me." As I spoke the words, visions of Mom floated into my head. It wasn't about letting go this time; I couldn't. This wasn't a person who'd suffered a disease where death was imminent. This was someone, an idea, a hope, a picture of strength that I somehow willed into being. How did I do that? Out of despair and the absolute stubborn belief that people dying wasn't the end, that somehow I could make it be about more.

But it wasn't.

Even so, Ana wasn't going. Some way, somehow, she wasn't dying. At least not without a fight.

The Omegans gathered us into small groups and marched us toward giant transport ships where they loaded us like cattle. A few got rambunctious and tried to resist but were quickly silenced with blows to their bodies. They removed our weapons and gear. A fleet of transport ships began to arrive and several people were loaded onto them.

Norg muttered, "Charista's just bought herself time, that's all."

"If the Failsafe is tied to the Valkyrie, she won't have much time at all."

"She'll get hers in time, and hopefully from us," Norg said. "I need me some Grade A payback, and I'm ready to pull the trigger on her."

"First things first. They're loading us and we'll need to size up things." I shuddered as I heard words that Baudricort or even Ana would be saying but they came from me. Treg and Norg looked at me for a moment with awe.

"We're open to suggestions, Nelson; you just keep that going." Treg grinned.

Norg steadied me. "Can't do anything now. Too many of them here. Better wait until it's a one on one thing."

"I'm wondering if they even know about me."

Norg eyed the Omegans. "I can't say for sure, but in any case, you get those Pulls you were talking about, best keep them quiet for now. We got to figure out our new situation and any advantage we got better be secret."

Norg and Treg remained back with the rest of us. Treg came closer and knelt by Ana; his eyes were shrouded in tears, and a deep wince hung on his face as he looked on her. "Anything from her?"

"Nothing."

"They won't take her with us," Norg said.

"Why not?" I asked.

"Heard some talkin'. They ain't no hospital. Anyone going with them's gotta be able to stand on their own. They're looking for slaves, not patients." Norg kicked the ground and grunted in disgust.

I shuddered at what else that meant. I cupped her head in my hand as a sob choked its way out of me. "They better kill me too then; I won't leave her like this."

I shook her body. Tears came loose and wandered down my face, splashing onto her chest. "Come on, you can't do this. You've got to live, Ana. You aren't ready for this; there's more you have to do. Please, just don't leave me. I need you. I've always needed you. Please."

Even the thoughts of returning home escaped me. What? Was that my home anymore? Had I lost everything that made me who I was? Was I still even Nelson? Was this where I belonged now?

For the first time, I heard a strain of emotion in Norg's voice. "We ain't going quietly, Prophet Man, I can assure you. I'm thinking of something."

"Looks to be now." Treg flashed a dagger in his hand. I grabbed for the dagger Ana held and nodded to him. "One or None, right?"

"Fuck-n A."

I watched the Omegans corral the Action and Coalition troops, and then Llewyn appeared. He walked with some of them and made comments.

Llewyn stood with the Omegans in a conference with Charista where it was laid out. The deal, the transfer. Llewyn watched us all, the sweat collected on his brow. My hands clenched into fists and, despite Treg's warning, I launched to my feet. The Omegans didn't grab me until I had a hand on him.

"What did you do? What is this?"

"It's survival; you wouldn't understand."

"Oh, I think I would. Only my version doesn't involve tossing people to the wolves."

"I won't debate the merits of this with you."

"Because there are none."

"Look, it's over, it's done, I made a deal." He turned, but I yanked him back and gazed into his eyes.

"You sold us like a bill of goods."

"We had to stop them; there was no other way."

"What about Cataclysm?"

"It's halfway to Lebabolis by now."

"You let them in on that little tidbit?"

He just eyed me in response.

"Was that even true, what Charista said about the Pox and curing the people?"

"They were able to mask the symptoms, but the disease has too good a stronghold. I must admit, Charista really didn't think that one through. All the while trying to come up with a weapon to attack, she created the greatest one ever. All from an accident."

"How long do they have?"

"Can't say, but you might as well break the news to Varrick's dear sister over there, if she ever comes around."

"Llewyn, what were you even thinking? What the hell did they even offer you to get you to consider anything this stupid?"

"It's not what they offered, it's what Charista offered. A place, status. Baudricort never saw the point of working with people. It was a good thing I killed him when I did."

"You son of a bitch."

"It was either him or all of us under a pile of rubble. Think these people will stop?"

"I think we'll never know now. We had a shot, a good one, and you gave it up for a safe bet and a deal with someone who wants to dismantle this planet. You're a worthless human being, and you're everything that was wrong with the Omegan experiment. They brought back humans, but I see they didn't weed out the assholes this time."

"Be that as it may, I don't expect we'll be speaking much anymore."

"How do you think? Who's to say I won't be able to use my mind about this place? It's served me pretty well so far."

"It has, but tell me, have you noticed anything different lately? That device keeps you stable, but it has also disconnected you. Nelson, I'm afraid you won't be planning or doing much of anything anymore. This world, your world, is no longer. The Omegans will take their control and agree to split the land with Lebabolis. There'll be the peace."

"You made deals with homicidal and ruthless creatures. And you're naive enough to think they'll play nice now that you've divided the sandbox up equally? I think we will be seeing each other again, and I really hope it's with me or someone else pointing a rifle at your chest."

"Save your strength, Nelson, the Omegan work camps are rather rigorous, or so I'm told."

I was about to launch into another tirade, but an Omegan stopped me short with a jab to my midsection. As Treg collected me from the floor, Llewyn finished and spoke with the Emperor for a while. Charista was on the screen and joined in their conversation. The deals of the terms were simple: we were all to be hauled away to their fortress. The peace was to be established. Omegans took their share of Valentium, Llewyn's fake ruse was just about preparing it and making a signal. The Omegans honed in on the Valentium as a waypoint to get to the Range. Cataclysm remained a mystery. None of the Omegans spoke about it, which worried me all the more. I wondered if they even knew about it. Unless they figured it was a secret that we didn't know about. They must have wondered about that fight back then, and how they were turned back so decisively after being able to get the best of the humans for so long.

And now I understood how the humans came. Like seeds collected from a harvest years back, planted and cultivated for one purpose. But they neglected to think about one key ingredient in the mix. The one thing that sets us apart. The ability to think, to choose. And they couldn't stop that, even after who knows what kind of conditioning and chemical treatments. They'd separated humans into products, and Lebabolis carried that vision over. But they wanted their own piece of the world, apart from the Omegans. And that was the struggle. I knew they wouldn't rest with this deal. Charista had a short time left for herself if she couldn't get her great big gun to work.

Norg neared me. "What's up, Prophet Man?"

"Not much, and all of it bad."

"Yeah, no kidding. We gotta play this cool and let Ana heal."

"What if she doesn't, Norg?"

"Don't even talk like that. We gotta think this through. When we get wherever we're going, we need to figure out our deal. Maybe Kado can help."

"If they don't grab him up and pick his brain first. I'm sure Llewyn gave them the dirty dark about each and every one of us. Surprised they aren't trying some kind of Link on me right now."

"Ana's gone?" Norg's eyes showed more emotion in that one statement than I'd ever seen. His lip twitched so fast I'd have sworn I was seeing things if I hadn't looked right at it then. He took a few slow breaths and shook his head. "Can't be, man. Just can't be. The Circle can't lose her. I—we can't lose her."

Her hair was strewn across her face, and her cheeks were ashen. It was easy for me to be worried about her, and I thought about Jacobs' remark. Maybe I had gotten attached to her. The sight of her, still as can be, wrecked my soul. Was this it? Was this her end? Why wasn't it more of a deal? Why weren't people around her, doing anything medically to save her? She deserved more than this.

The feelings thrashed around in me, wanting to grab her and shake her, do whatever came to mind in my infinite lack of medical knowledge that was only supplemented by medical TV dramas. There was nothing I could do. Kado was gone, and there wasn't anyone who either could help or was able to right then. I'd seen this all too recently and, while we had no blood connection, this was worse in some bizarre way.

Her high cheekbones were tainted with smudges of dirt and dried blood. She was so full of energy, so full of life. I imagined her about, standing and commanding, rolling her eyes at one of my jokes, anything. But there she lay, like a mannequin that had never been alive.

Then, before I realized it happened, her hand jumped and clasped my wrist, and my heart felt like it had stopped beating. I forgot to breathe and watched Norg. Moisture formed at the corner of his eye; the only other thing he did was grunt and shake. A sharp piercing shock ripped through me, and my heart about burst through my mouth.

Ana took a gasp, and the rest of us fell back. Her brow immediately crinkled again, and a low moan escaped her lips. She blinked her eyes and they opened slowly. She winced.

I watched in amazement and hoped I hadn't imagined this, that this wasn't what had been happening with the Pull and the maps and the strange words. Once I saw Treg's and Norg's faces, I knew what I saw wasn't fake or in my head.

It was real; she was still here.

Treg was the first who found words. "Hey, Ana, you there?"

She squirmed in pain. Her eyes swiveled around. Her voice came in a scratchy whisper. "Mmm, yeah, think so. What happened?"

"Just about everything bad you can imagine," Norg offered.

"Well, that's typical." She wheezed and coughed. A splash of blood hit her lip. "Where are we?"

"The Range. Llewyn sold us out."

"What?"

"The deal, the package. It's us."

Ana heaved. "D-damn prick. Never liked his ass. What'd he get?"

"Not sure, but it sounds like he was pulling for Lebabolis all along. Surprised Baudricort didn't know about it, or let on if he did. Llewyn was the one who killed him all this time later."

"Why?"

"Charista. She made him a deal like she made one with us. Now we know what that's worth."

"They've got Kado. Do we have time?"

"Dunno."

"What about the Guard?"

"They wasted a lot of 'em. Don't know about the others."

"Don't count on 'em." Ana took a labored breath. "It's just us now. They wouldn't even listen to me at the Valkyrie."

"We were in a tough spot; we didn't have a whole lot of choices."

"And now looks like we have none."

"No, but look what we got." Ana raised a shaky hand and pointed at each of us around her. "We'll figure it out." She grimaced but propped herself up after a little effort. A steady trickle of blood oozed from her mouth.

"You sure you're alright?" I asked.

"Ow." She went into a heaving fit but managed to add, "I'll live, I think."

"Doesn't sound too convincing. Stick close to me; I'll keep an eye on you." I clasped her shoulder. She watched me with worried eyes but managed a nod in response.

I breathed the deep sigh I'd held for some time. She was alive, and like the rest of us, she had a chance. And for Ana Crucinal, that's all she ever needed.

Get the Rest of the Story

Have you read "Cataclysm Epoch"? It's book 1 of the Valkyrie Chronicles Series and is available on Amazon.com in Kindle and print formats!

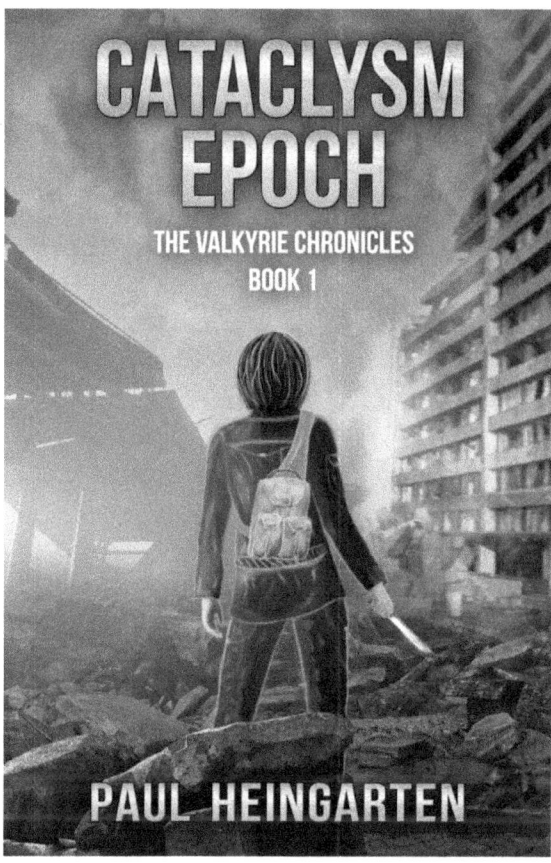

Ana Crucinal is on the run from Lebabolis, the nation that sprung up in a world ravaged from its last and most devastating war. She is with the Action, the ragtag group of rebels who fight against everything Lebabolis stands for.

Ana joins a mission to cross time to retrieve a man named Xander Lee who everyone believes is the author of the world they live in. But can Xander be convinced what they're saying is true and will they be able to get him to come back to the future with them?

Will Ana save her sick brother while trying to get Xander to come through time for her?

Get the Rest of the Story

Did you like "Settling Darkness"? How would you like to receive future novels from me for FREE? Go to my website at www.paulheingarten.com and click on the "Krewe of Paul (VIP)" link for more information.

About the Author

Paul Heingarten spreads time between writing, being a musician, and, since 2002, a career in Information Technology. He lives in the southern United States with his wife Andrea. Settling Darkness is his third novel.

Other Titles by Paul Heingarten

The Harvest (short story)
Leave from Absence (novel)
The Monitor (short story)
Natural Election (short story)
Cataclysm Epoch (novel)